MICHELLE VERNAL LOVES a happy ending. She lives with her husband and their two boys in the beautiful and resilient city of Christchurch, New Zealand. She's partial to a glass of wine, loves a cheese scone, and has recently taken up yoga—a sight to behold indeed. As well as the Guesthouse on the Green series Michelle's written seven novels—they're all written with humour and warmth and she hopes you enjoy reading them. If you enjoy Christmas at O'Mara's then taking the time to say so by leaving a review would be wonderful. A book review is the best present you can give an author. If you'd like to hear about Michelle's new releases, you can subscribe to her Newsletter via her website at www.michellevernalbooks.com[1] and to say thank you, you'll receive an exclusive O'Mara women character profile!

Also by Michelle Vernal

The Cooking School on the Bay
Second-hand Jane
Staying at Eleni's
The Traveller's Daughter
Sweet Home Summer
The Promise
When We Say Goodbye
And...
Introducing: The Guesthouse on the Green Series
Book 1 - O'Mara's
Book 2 – Moira-Lisa Smile
Book 3 – What Goes on Tour
Book 4 – Rosi's Regrets

Christmas at O'Mara's
By Michelle Vernal

Introduction

C liona Whelan, Clio for short, had been many things in her fifty-nine years on this earth. A daughter, a sister, an aunt, a friend, journalist and now a published and, some would say, feted novelist, but there were things she hadn't been too. Things she'd have liked to have been had fate played her a different hand. If she'd been born into these modern times, perhaps she would have had it all but in her youth, there was no such thing as, "having your cake and eating it too". She'd had to make choices, hard decisions because she couldn't have it all. She wasn't a wife, nor a mother and she would never be someone's grandmother. 'I've got you though haven't I, Bess.' It was a statement not a question and she reached down to stroke the cat's silky back as she meandered past on her way through from the kitchen where she'd finished her breakfast to bask on her favourite chair. Bess mewled but didn't pause on her well-worn path.

Clio took a sip of milky tea from her china cup. The dancing rose pattern, so delicate against the white, bone china, was beautiful and she paused briefly to admire it as she set it back down in its matching saucer. The Japanese knew the importance of things being just right when it came to drinking one's tea. They'd understand her refusal to sip her morning brew from anything other than this rose teacup. It was a habit adopted from her mam. God rest her soul. 'It tastes different when it's not in my cup,' Maeve Whelan used to say. Clio had thought her a terrible old fusspot suffering from delusions of grandeur when she was young, but now, she knew exactly what she'd meant.

She heard the familiar rattle of the cast iron letter slot being pushed open by Niall. He of the ruddy cheeks and ready grin who'd been the postman delivering to her street for forever and a day. It was followed by the soft plop of mail landing on the mat by the front door. Clio liked this time of year. Oh, she wasn't a fan of the cold. She'd have been happier banging away on her trusty old typewriter somewhere warm and sunny like Spain. Dublin could be bleak in the depth of winter. What she liked about the month of December though, was the way in which people became kinder and more engaged with one another. Those that would hurry along the streets, heads down, keen to be on their way the rest of the year, would slow a little, look one another in the eye and give a nodding smile in passing. It was as if they'd suddenly remembered what really mattered in life. She enjoyed sifting through the post of a morning too knowing there'd be a pile of cards to open—it was much more enjoyable than eyeing the electric bill while munching her toast.

Clio liked to eke out her morning routine, partly because it took longer to wind through the gears and crank into fourth these days and partly because she wasn't, and never had been, a morning person. She got up and knotted her dressing gown tie before padding through on slipper-clad feet to the kitchen. She slotted her toast into the toaster pushing the handle down before going to fetch the mail. The white envelopes lay scattered on the floor and her eyes flitted over the different handwriting as she scooped them up, but as she registered the postmark on one such envelope her breath caught and her hand fluttered to her mouth. The envelope, as her eyes drifted to the lazy, looping script she'd never expected to see again, seemed to vibrate in her hand. It was nonsensical she knew. Her heart, she realised, had begun to race in a way she should perhaps at her age find alarming but the doctor had told her just last week her ticker was strong as an ox.

'Go and sit down, Clio,' she ordered and with the envelope pulsing on top of the small pile she'd swept up, that's what she did. She pushed her glasses onto the bridge of her nose and pinched her bottom lip between her teeth as she retrieved the letter opener from the dish on the table. Then, sliding it through the crisp white paper, she retrieved the card inside. The last correspondence she'd had from him had been a letter written on a sheet of notepaper. That was forty-one years ago, although, if you were to ask her, she could tell you exactly where that letter could be found. This card, she saw inspecting it, was rather nondescript, an expensive looking nativity picture, a slightly different version of the same scenes already draped over the string she'd tied around one curtain finial stretching it across to the other as she did each year to dangle her cards from.

She wondered if he'd spent time in the newsagent's loitering for an age by the rack of Christmas cards trying to decide which to choose, in the end playing it safe and settling on something rather stock standard. Or, perhaps it had simply come from a packet of ten, selected at random from the choice of Santa Claus with his sack of presents, a Christmas tree or the nativity scene. Nerves were making her procrastinate because it wasn't the image on the front that mattered, it was what the card said inside. 'Go on, Clio, old girl. Since when you were afraid of anything? Open it.' She did so.

Chapter 1
London, December 21, 1999

Roisin O'Mara was not feeling festive. In fact, she was feeling decidedly foul and full of fecks as with her free hand she closed the gate. It clanged shut with a force threatening to snap it off its hinges. The plastic bag with the presents she was carting banged against her leg as she stomped up the path to the front door. Its green colour was a beacon on a day that was threatening more snow and she sent a flurry of the sludgy stuff that had settled overnight flying as her feet skidded on the icy surface. 'Fecking, Colin,' she muttered, her breath coming in huffy, white puffs. You'd have thought he'd have swept the path for them. Mind you, she shouldn't be surprised. Considerate had never been a word that sprang to mind when she thought about her estranged husband. She was beginning to agree with her sister Moira, Arse was a much more fitting term for Colin Quealey.

Sure, a girl could fall over and do an injury on this path, she griped silently. 'Watch your step, Noah.' Her son was in a hurry to reach the house and she'd rather he made it there intact. They were late, which wasn't helping her mood because she knew their tardy arrival would be noted with a sniff. Her soon to be ex-mother-in-law, Elsa, was the queen of the disapproving sniff. The annoying thing was it wasn't even her fault. They'd left their tiny flat in a leafy, overpriced pocket of Greenwich in plenty of time but her old banger had protested against the cold by refusing to start. Her language, muttered under her breath, had been ripe as she turned the key for the umpteenth time knowing she was in danger of flooding the engine. She'd been about to tell Noah to unbuckle because they'd have to go back inside and ring Daddy to ask him to pick them up when she'd given it one last try. She'd sent a "thank you" heavenward as the engine spluttered into life.

The traffic despite the busy time of year had been light on the drive over. Roisin was guessing most people had the sense to hunker down for the day than to venture out and about. She envied them, she'd thought, turning into Staunton Mews ten minutes later. It was the sort of Sunday that should be spent in pyjamas, snuggling under a duvet on the couch watching videos while stuffing one's face, not partaking in a farcical Christmas day with whatever you called your mother-in-law and husband once you'd pulled the pin on your marriage.

She'd managed to slide into a parking space a few doors down from number nine and even though she'd only walked from the car to the path her feet were already icicles inside her boots. This was despite her having worn socks so thick over her black tights she knew her boots would be pinching before the day was out.

Oh yes, this two Christmas day's lark was a pain in the arse and she'd have rather left Colin, Elsa and Noah to the goose that was undoubtedly on the menu but Elsa had other plans. She'd been insistent she come, giving a loud sniff before remonstrating, 'It's important to present a united front you know, Roisin. That poor boy deserves a proper Christmas with both his parents given everything he's been through.'

Roisin knew she wasn't being overly sensitive—there was a definite accusatory tone in Elsa Quealey's voice. She'd been tempted to point out that her son had played a lead role in their marriage disintegrating too. Elsa seemed to have forgotten all about the bank having foreclosed on them, selling their home and assets to clear debts Colin had amassed, unbeknown to his wife, with his ill-fated, investments. This was why Roisin and Noah now lived in a flat the size of a shoebox and why she drove a temperamental car that would have been right at home cruising the streets back in nineteen seventy-one. It was also why her husband at the ripe old age of thirty-nine had slunk home to lick his wounds at his mother's house. She'd have dearly loved to have rubbed Elsa's nose in all of this as she looked down that long beak of hers waiting for her to say yes to her Christmas dinner invitation.

It rankled too the reference to 'poor Noah'. He was doing fine. Sure, the first wee while had been rough as he adjusted to all the changes their separation wrought, but of late he'd settled down and was back to his usual, happy self, pestering her constantly for a gerbil. He hadn't shut up about it, in fact. He'd forgotten all about wanting Mummy and Daddy to live together in their old house again because becoming the owner of a small, furry brown rodent was the number one priority in his life.

Roisin's friend Stephanie had warned her not to go there and she was inclined to agree, as was her landlord, who'd enunciated loudly—he was hard of hearing—that no animals were allowed. Was a gerbil an animal? Roisin wasn't sure but it was a good excuse to appease Noah, so she'd run with it. 'They look small and innocuous enough,' Stephanie had said. 'You could even say they're quite sweet looking but Rosi think about the havoc Charlie caused bringing Beyoncé to school on pet day.'

Roisin had nodded. She well remembered the story of Stephanie's daughter's gerbil escaping and terrorising the head-mistress by hiding out in the toilets. Still, the look on Noah's face when he'd asked whether she thought Father Christmas would get his letter in time because there was NOTHING he wanted more in the world than a gerbil and he'd been ever such a good boy had made her waiver. Perhaps she could get away with a soft toy version. Ah, who was she kidding?

That's what she needed to remember, she told herself look-ing down at her son. Today was about him, not her, and besides if she hadn't agreed to come then Colin might have put his foot down regarding her spending Christmas day proper with her family in Dublin. They'd yet to iron out all the nitty gritty finer points of custody where their son was concerned but seemed to have settled into an unspoken arrangement whereby, he spent every second weekend with his daddy and Granny Quealey.

Her son's hat was pulled down low and he was dwarfed in-side the jacket Colin had bought him a few weeks ago despite his proclamations of trying to get back on his feet and that the maintenance he was currently paying out was daylight robbery. There'd been nothing wrong with Noah's old jacket but Colin was a show pony, always had been and appearances mattered to him. She could sense, despite his five-year-old body being hid-den inside an expensive layer of goose down, Noah twitching with an energetic excitement at the thought of what lay in wait for him inside Granny Quealey's house. Throw in some sugary treats that were bound to be coming his way very soon and he'd be bouncing off the walls in no time.

That was another thing, she thought, a gloved finger pressing the doorbell and holding it down for longer than was necessary; those weekends spent here saw Noah get spoiled rotten. He'd burst in through the door of their small flat on a Sunday afternoon full of stories about ice creams and trips to the cinema. She felt as though she were in a competition for her son's affections, one in which not only the financial odds were stacked against her but the opportunity to simply relax and have fun with him too. What annoyed her most of all and yes, she knew it was irrational but she couldn't help how she felt was Elsa serving him up chicken nuggets and chips, his all-time favourite. Her son was very quick to point out that she didn't put anything green on his plate to ruin his dinner either. He'd say this while waving a piece of broccoli at her in an accusatory fashion. Colin would have told her off when they were still living under the same roof if she'd put an unbalanced meal like that in front of Noah. Would he say "boo" to his mother, though? No, he would not.

Their roles had changed since they'd parted ways. He it seemed, got to play at being jolly, good time daddy every second weekend, something he'd never been good at before but seemed to be hitting his stride with now, while she did the day to day parenting hard yards. It wasn't fair.

Her mood darkened as she jiggled inside her coat waiting for the door to open. She'd never breathe a word about how their new arrangement made her feel to Colin because his face would scrunch up in that annoying pinched way it did when something pained him and he'd say, 'Well, Roisin, it wasn't my decision to separate nor is it my fault Noah has to split his time between his parents.' He'd be right too, it had been her decision and not one she'd taken lightly. She and Colin had not been a good match. It was also one, despite her and Noah's flat with its moaning and groaning pipes and dodgy hot water, she didn't regret. 'Hurry up,' she muttered, her breath emitting another puff of white into the air.

'You look like you're smoking, Mummy.' Noah grinned revealing two new front teeth finally beginning to grow down. His lisp was still pronounced though. He reached over and snapped a twig from the spindly hydrangea in the front garden.

'What are you doing?'

Noah didn't get a chance to answer because the door swung open to reveal Elsa Quealey. The smile on her face drooped as she took in the sight of her beloved grandson holding a twig between his fingers and sucking on it as though his life depended on it.

Chapter 2

'What are you doing, Noah?' Elsa frowned, watching as he exhaled a white plume into the air with the kind of satisfied gusto reserved for those that had just done the deed.

'Smoking like Mummy.'

'Noah, I don't smoke.' Roisin was indignant.

'No, but it looked like you were, Mummy.'

Elsa shook her grey chin-length hair which was as inflexible as she was, thanks to the liberal misting of Elnett hairspray each morning. Roisin watched her lips purse signalling disapproval and it made her think of a cat's arse. Jaysus, she was really getting into the swing of things, Roisin thought, giving her Christmas finery the once over as they were swept in from the cold. Elsa had teemed her handknitted red reindeer sweater with a pair of fat twin Santa Clauses dangling from her ear lobes. As the front door was closed behind her, Roisin's sense of smell was assaulted simultaneously with the aroma of roasting goose and her mother-in-law's heady floral fragrance, Joy. She'd be a nightmare to get stuck in a lift with, Roisin had often thought, sure you'd suffocate from the fumes coming off her before anyone come to the rescue.

'Shoes off, Noah, please,' Roisin bossed as Elsa busied herself unwrapping him and hanging his coat up on the hooks by the door leaving her to stamp the snow off her boots and shrug out of her coat. She felt very un-Christmassy compared to her mother-in-law in her plain grey wrap dress. It had seemed simple and stylish when she'd put it on that morning, the perfect outfit for a date with her ex-husband and his mother, nothing flashy, no hint of cleavage or thigh to be disapproved over, but now it just seemed drab. She fluffed her hair up knowing the woolly hat she'd pulled on would have flattened it.

'Colin's just on a business call. He works so hard that boy, he never stops,' Elsa said, herding them into the front room. 'The fire's roaring. Go and warm yourselves up. I've just got to baste the goose and then I'll bring some light refreshments through. I'll be back in a jiffy.'

You'd think she was entertaining the landed gentry, Roisin thought. It was going to be a long day. She poked her head back out the door and called out, 'I feel terrible arriving empty handed. I would've been happy to bring a dessert or a bottle of wine.' The older woman had been insistent she not bring anything and the bag of begrudged presents she was clutching didn't count. Elsa's sprightly form didn't falter as she marched down the hall waving the comment away.

'Nonsense, Roisin, I always think homemade is so much nicer than shop bought and Colin has a good nose for wine.'

Roisin mouthed, 'Bitch,' behind her back and Colin had a fecking big conker, that's what he had, *nose for wine my arse*. She stood still for a moment and breathed in slowly through her nostrils then exhaled in a slow hiss through her mouth just as she did in her yoga sessions. She was a long way from feeling mindful but it did unknot the twisted feeling her mother-in-law was so adept at bringing out in her.

'Mummy, look at the tree!'

It was real of course, Roisin thought, turning to admire it. It was standing proudly in its bucket giving off a gorgeous scent of pine which was mingling with the woodsmoke from the crackling fire in the hearth. The house had central heating and Elsa only got the fire going on special occasions but there really was something inviting about an open fire, and she looked at the flames leap and dance for a second before turning her attention back to the tree and her son who was squealing with delight at the packages laid out around it.

The decorations dripped from the green fronds which bowed under the weight of them despite the sturdy branches. Roisin knew amongst all the tinsel and baubles were the ornaments Colin would have hung. A new one bought for each of his birthdays. It was a tradition Elsa was carrying on with Noah and five would be set aside for him to place on the tree today. She felt a pang, thinking about the measly fake excuse for a fir tree brought on a rushed trip to Argos earlier in the week. She'd poked it in the corner of their flat trying not to feel let down by its lacklustre appearance which seemed to scream, 'I couldn't be arsed!'. There'd been no point in sourcing a real tree though, not with them heading over to Dublin tomorrow.

She'd done her best to make decorating it fun, popping on the Christmas CD she always played this time of year. Christmas wasn't Christmas without a bit of Band Aid and she did so love doing the Simon le Bon bit. She'd straightened its sparse wire branches, getting Noah to unearth his favourite trimmings from the old suitcase she'd brought with them from their old house. They'd whiled away all of five minutes dressing it, and Noah had asked, as he hung the wooden gingerbread man he'd painted when he was three, if the tree was sick. 'Mummy, it really doesn't look very well you know.'

He was right and as she'd stood back to look at their handiwork she'd sighed. She could hear Mammy in her ear and knew exactly what she'd say if she was there, 'You can't make a silk purse out of a sow's ear, Roisin.' Feeling Noah's eyes on her she'd been tempted to tell him that sometimes in life you got what you paid for but he didn't need to know that, not yet anyway. So, instead she told him she thought the tree might be suffering from tinselitis. He'd whiled away a good hour after that with his little red doctor's kit. Yes, even dripping with Christmassy embellishments their Argos special came a very poor second to this majestic fir tree that had taken up residence in the Quealeys' front room. The sheer size of it rivalled Enid Blyton's Faraway tree. If only she could clamber up it and escape through the cloud at the top to the land of anywhere but here.

She remembered the bag of gifts she'd bought. There was a bar of Joy soap for Elsa—she couldn't stretch to an actual bottle this year but the Boots' girl had assured her the soap was a triple milled, French luxury that wouldn't turn to sludge as it sat beside the bath. There was the usual bottle of malt whisky for Colin and, just because she wanted her presence registered under the tree where Noah was concerned today, a box of Lego. The bloody stuff cost a fortune and should come with a health warning for parents to always wear shoes once opened she'd griped, wrapping it when her son had been brushing his teeth earlier that morning.

'Here, Noah, put these under the tree.' He was already on his hands and knees inspecting the labels on the cheerily wrapped packages leaning against the bucket and ignored the rustle of plastic she set down next to him. He picked one up and prodded at it, a frown of concentration on his face. It was mean the way Elsa always made him wait until after lunch to open his presents. She was a stickler for her traditions and Roisin knew the drill. There would be drinks and nibbles first, followed by a lunch far too big for the four of them, then it would be back here where Noah could finally rip into his presents before doling out the rest of the gifts. Then, it would be time for a game of charades followed by coffee, served in the silver plunger which, like the fire, was reserved for special occasions, and finally a film. The Quality Street would be produced with a flourish but a beady eye would be kept on those attempting to take more than one at a time. Roisin sighed at the thought of it all. She planned on making their escape by four thirty which was the earliest they could politely do so. This would give her enough time to pack for their flight in the morning.

The thought of her mammy and sisters lifted her, she was looking forward to seeing them. It had been over two months since they'd last all been together and although she spoke to one of them every other day it wasn't the same as being there amongst it all. So much had happened since she'd returned from that last trip to Dublin, a newly separated woman who had to somehow find a new life for herself in London. Her brain was still whirring with it all but she hadn't looked back, not once.

Mammy of course had been insistent on meeting them at the airport and that she and Noah come to her in Howth when they arrived. The thing was, her new apartment chosen for its seaside location wasn't O'Mara's. The apartment on the top floor of the family guesthouse was home. Roisin wanted to be back in her old room, to join in with the bickering between

Moira and Aisling. Truth be told she'd have given anything to have Mammy and Daddy back under that roof too, but time didn't stand still and things had changed with Daddy's passing. She didn't blame Mammy for moving, she could understand the need for a new beginning after her life had been thrown off course.

Mammy had done the hard sell and would have given any estate agent a run for their money as she emphasised her apartment's seaside location and stunning views. To which Rosie had replied, given the time of year the water was fit for polar bears not people, come to that it was pretty much the same in summertime too. In the end it was decided they'd stay that first night at Mammy's and then play it by ear.

She wondered what the Christmas tree in the foyer of O'Mara's looked like and smiled at the thought of Aisling and Bronagh, the guesthouse's long serving receptionist, arguing over whether they should go with a silver and gold theme. Bronagh had won, Aisling had told her, adding that fair play to her it did look gorgeous albeit enormous. It couldn't be bigger than the one she was standing here looking at though, surely? Either way she was looking forward to seeing it for herself. Yes, she thought, hugging her arms around herself, it would be nice to be back in Dublin, like putting on a pair of comfy slippers. She twiddled her toes, the fecking boots were already beginning to pinch.

To distract herself from her squished toes, Roisin did a sweep of the room, noting the tidily arranged cards on the mantle. Her eyes moved to the sideboard and she saw the Royal Doulton ballerina and the collection of porcelain Beatrix Potter figurines that normally adorned it had been put away.

When Noah had been a toddler, Jemima Puddleduck and her friends had been like a magnet to him and she'd been terrified he'd break one of them. The more she'd told him not to touch the more determined he'd been to do just that. In their place was a faux gingerbread house, a red glow emanating from inside its white trimmed windows and next to it was a nativity scene, the small wooden figures, Roisin knew, having once belonged to Elsa's mother.

'Roisin, Merry Christmas. You're looking well.' Colin intruded on her inspection as he appeared in the doorway, the joviality in his tone sounding forced to her ears but she gave him ten out of ten for effort. Registering her normally staid suit-wearing ex was dressed in a navy version of his mother's reindeer sweater she choked back a giggle. Elsa had him well and truly under the thumb. He was also wearing jeans, and not very well. He was one of those men who never looked comfortable in denim. Come to that he didn't look comfortable in anything casual, it wasn't his style. An awkwardness hovered in the air as they both pondered the best way in which to greet one another. Roisin decided to run with formal which while strange felt more honest than an effusive hug and kiss hello. 'Merry Christmas, Colin.'

He homed in and gave her a peck on the cheek, his lips dry and cool as they grazed her skin. She inhaled his familiar Armani aftershave and for a moment she was tempted to grasp hold of him, to be back where everything was familiar, but she steeled herself. Just because something was familiar and easy didn't mean it was good for you, and besides, she'd done the hardest bit, the actual leaving, and look how far she'd come. No, there was no going back. Still, she acknowledged as he took a step back and ruffled Noah's hair, it was sad how it had all worked out. They'd both gone into their marriage full of hope and look where they were now.

'Thank you for coming,' he said as Noah wrapped himself around his father's legs. There was a time Colin would have been irritated by his son's playful affection but since they'd separated, he seemed to appreciate these gestures more. There was always a silver lining, Rosin mused, and she smiled back at him. He hadn't needed to say that, he was making an effort and so would she. 'The tree's a beauty.'

'Mummy wanted the biggest we could find.'

But it was going to be hard.

Chapter 3

'Noah if you shake that any more whatever is inside the wrapping paper will be in a million little pieces by the time you get to open it.'

Noah looked at his mother, the frustration evident on his face and she felt a tug on her heartstrings. 'Could he not just open one before lunch, Colin?' she whispered, watching him pick up another parcel. 'We don't need to tell Elsa.'

Colin looked at her aghast. Her ex-husband was a rule breaker in the business world where he seemed to think they didn't apply to him but when it came to the rules laid down by his mother, he might as well have been the same age as his son.

Roisin sighed and managed to inject some steel in her tone. 'Put it down, Noah.'

He did so, sitting back on his haunches and crossing his arms sulkily.

'Colin, can you get the door for me?' Elsa's voice trilled from the hallway and Colin moved toward it. She appeared with a tray, upon which three steaming goblets of mulled wine, a stick of cinnamon peeking over each of the rims, were perched along with an orange juice for Noah. It was proper juice with bits in it which for some strange reason was his favourite.

'Elsa, let me take that for you.' Roisin remembered her manners.

'I can manage, thank you.' She placed the tray down on the coffee table. 'But you could be a dear and go and get the mince pies for me. There's a plate on the worktop in the kitchen.'

'Of course. Noah, you're not to wander about with that juice, do you hear me?' His sulk over the presents was forgotten and he nodded as Elsa perched down on the sofa next to Colin. She left them to it and headed up the hallway, the walls of which were adorned with photographs of Colin at varying ages. She paused as she always did to smirk up at the last one, taken in his final year at high school. His face was spotty with adolescence and he looked like he was being strangled by his school tie. It was his hair that made her laugh though. It was hard to imagine her husband had ever idolised anybody other than himself but in that old pic he was rocking his curly mullet and had clearly been a fan of Hall & Oates. A tiny sign of re-bellion because she was betting Elsa had pestered him day and night to get to the barber shop for a short back and sides. Colin's dad had passed away when he was small and she used to wonder what Colin would have been like if Elsa had had some-one else to fuss over in their family dynamic.

She pulled herself away from the photograph and followed her nose into the kitchen which despite the preparations was in an orderly state with neatly stacked dishes. It was the opposite of the last Christmas spent in Dublin two years ago now when the dishes had haphazardly been piled so high, an avalanche of china was a very real threat. There'd been the usual arguing over who'd been put in charge of the roasty potatoes and who'd left the cabbage stewing. She could hear Moira proclaiming the pot of boiled greens smelt like a urinal and the memory made her grin. Mammy had thwacked her with the wooden spoon for that one.

She might not be a fan of goose but it did smell good and as she inhaled her tummy rumbled. The potatoes she saw, lifting a lid off one of the pots on the stove, were waiting to be parboiled before being tossed in the goose fat and cooked until they'd transformed into crunchy roast taties. The Brussel sprouts were ready to be put on along with the carrots and peas. Colin was terrible on the baby cabbages but it wasn't her that would have to put up with the aftermath all evening, not this year. The thought buoyed her and she picked up the mince pies, home-made of course with a dusting of icing sugar over the top of them, and carried them back through to the front room.

Noah was just hanging the last of his special decorations on the tree and as she stood in the doorway he began entertaining his granny and daddy with tales about Beyoncé the gerbil. He lived vicariously through Charlotte when it came to that gerbil of hers, she thought, wavering on her stance of not buying him a pet for Christmas. He loved that bloody gerbil and he thought of Charlie as an honorary sister ever since they'd stayed with Stephanie and Jeffrey after she and Colin had separated, lisping to her often that she was annoying, just like a real sister. She had a lot to thank the Wentworth-Islington-Greene's for. If they hadn't opened up their home to her and Noah she may well have come knocking on Elsa's door with her tail between her legs. Stephanie had helped her find her way at a time when she'd felt really, rather lost.

It was Jeffery who'd wrangled a position for her at the enormous accountancy firm in which he was a senior partner. She was now secretary for twenty-five hours of the week to Nor-

man who really did look like a Norman with his little round
glasses, small build and shiny domed head. She wasn't a very
good secretary but she was trying and Norman was a very kind
hearted man so, they were rubbing along nicely. Stephanie had
helped her source her flat which while tiny was in the right location and meant Noah didn't have to change schools. She'd
even started doing her yoga teacher training and the other
night when she'd gotten up to draw the curtains and seen a star
shooting across the inky sky, she'd made a wish that one day
soon, she'd be in a position to open her own studio. For the first
time in her life Roisin had a plan and she was determined to
stick to it. Now as she stood on the periphery of the room, plate
of mince pies in hand she felt disconnected from the tableau. It
was a strange thought but it didn't make her sad.

'Roisin, what are doing standing there letting the cold air
in?' Elsa brought her back into the room.

'Sorry.' She pushed the door shut with her foot and put the
plate down on the coffee table.

'Noah,' Elsa said, 'come and sit up here now and have a
mince pie.' She gestured to the low slung Ercol chair. Elsa and
her late husband, Errol had bought the set of Ercol furniture
not long after they were married and she was very fond of saying, 'quality lasts you know'.

Noah who knew all about being naughty or nice at this
time of year decided to roll with nice. He had one more wistful
glance at the shiny wrapped boxes under the tree before sitting
down in the chair as his granny had asked him to do. Roisin
eyed him and was reminded of an old film, Little Lord
Fauntleroy. Her son knew which side his bread was buttered

on, that was for sure. She sat down in the matching chair opposite him.

'Now,' Elsa said doling out dainty china side plates and red serviettes. 'Watch what I do.' Roisin had the unnerving sensation she too was being given a lesson on how to eat a mince pie as Elsa flapped the red napkin before draping it over her lap. 'That way you'll catch any stray crumbs.'

Roisin quickly did the same, eager to get the show on the road and shove a mince pie in her gob. Colin was sitting straight backed, napkin in place, looking like he was waiting for his mother to pat him on the head and tell him he was a good boy. Her finger twitched with the urge to flip him the finger. He was such a goody-two shoes where Elsa was concerned, it had always annoyed her and still did, even now when it was no longer anything to do with her. She managed to keep her finger to herself moving her eyes away from him to watch as Noah set about demonstrating a strong future as a flag bearer with his napkin before finally draping it across his trousers. Elsa nodded approvingly before passing the plate around.

'Jesus, Mary and Joseph about time,' Roisin hissed between her teeth.

'Did you say something, dear?' Elsa glanced over, questioning eyebrow raised.

'Only that you make a lovely mince pie, Elsa.'

Elsa sniffed as a spray of crumbs shot forth unbidden from Roisin's mouth. Ah well, Roisin thought, Elsa had always thought her an uncouth Irish heathen. In for a penny in for a pound, she might as well knock the mulled wine back too.

She wished she hadn't when the spices, of which there were plenty, caught in the back of her throat. She felt it begin to close over a split second before she made a holy show of herself coughing and spluttering as though she were on her last legs.

'I'll get you some water.' Colin dashed off to pour her a glass and when he reappeared, she snatched it from him gratefully taking a big gulp only to cough once again and wind up with it dribbling down her chin and onto her dress. Fat lot of good, the fecking napkin was, she thought seeing the damp stain spread over the grey fabric. Her blurred vision cleared and she saw Noah staring at her wide eyed. *Ah, poor love*, she thought, *I frightened him*. 'I'm alright now, sweetheart,' she rasped, 'It just went down the wrong way that's all.' She refrained from adding his witch of a granny had probably deliberately loaded hers with mixed spice. She really wasn't feeling her usual sunny self because when her son piped up with, 'Well, Mummy, you always tell me not to drink too fast.' It took all her strength not to tell him to cork it if he knew what was good for him. At that moment he looked very much like a little version of his father. They were a bad influence these Quealeys so they were, she decided, finally getting her breathing back under control.

'Alright now?' Elsa had watched her carry-on with alarm.

'Mm,' she nodded. 'Sorry about that.'

So, Roisin, tell us how this new job of yours is going,' Elsa said and she saw Colin's ears perk up. She opened her mouth to tell them a funny story about how Norman had caught her in Proud Warrior stance in the empty boardroom during her lunchbreak, knowing they wouldn't be amused but determined to tell the tale anyway, but Elsa cut her off. 'I'm sure the reason Noah's only just shaken that dreadful cold is because of the afterschool programme you've put him in.'

If there'd been another mulled wine sitting on the table, she'd have picked that up and gulped it down.

Chapter 4

Somehow, Roisin managed to keep her composure as the hours dragged by. Once she'd moved on from her near death, mulled wine experience she dug deep and joined in with Elsa and Colin's joviality. This was their Christmas day, their special time with Noah and even if her mother-in-law or ex-mother-in-law or whatever she flipping was, had been a horrid old bite to her in the past, she loved her grandson. It was for this reason she kept the smile plastered to her face as she sat down for lunch at the dining table in the formal dining room. Elsa had handwritten name cards and Roisin saw she'd been placed at the far end of the table. If it was intended to make her feel like an afterthought then it had worked, she thought, sitting down. She concentrated on the table which was laid beautifully with a lacy white cloth and an elaborate holly centrepiece. A gold foil-wrapped Christmas cracker was lined up next to everyone's fork, soldier straight, and Noah was already fiddling with his when Roisin next looked up. 'Hold your horses, Noah, we'll pull them in a minute. This looks lovely, Elsa.' She wouldn't show the old witch she was annoyed at being plonked in the seating equivalent of Siberia.

Elsa preened as she disappeared, returning a moment later with a tureen full of vegetables. Colin brought up the rear with more bowls of food until at last, the pièce de résistance, the goose arrived swamped by golden potatoes. 'It smells wonderful doesn't it, Noah?' Her tummy churned at the thought of the gamey meat.

'Is it like Kentucky Fried Chicken? Because I like that.'

'No, not really but it's very tasty like Kentucky Fried Chicken.' She lied.

'Where's its head gone, Mummy?'

'Well, er...'

'And doesn't a goose have feathers and a big long neck like the one in my book. And, Mummy, why's it got an orange stuck up its—'

'Righty-ho.' Roisin clapped her hands. 'Would you like me to pour the wine?'

Colin looked at her like she'd grown another head which was what she'd expected, he always did the honours but at least it had gotten David Attenborough over there, off the topic of Mrs Goose's posterior. He set about playing host.

Elsa sat down next to Noah and waved her cracker at him. 'Shall we pull it?' A fierce look of competitiveness came over her son's face and it was mirrored back at him in his granny's. Roisin watched carefully. Noah's competitive streak came from the Quealey side and knowing how much Elsa liked to win, she wouldn't put it past her to pull the little card strip. She'd done it to her last year but Noah was only five and if she cheated there'd be tears. A tug-o-war ensued, teeth were set in grim determination, and Roisin sat with teeth clenched rooting for Noah. He was flung back in his seat at the cracker popped and *Yes!* victory was his. There was no graciousness in winning where he was concerned because you'd have thought he'd just got a gold medal for cracker pulling the way he was brandishing his prized half about. Roisin watched Elsa's lips press together in a thin, tight little line and was glad it was Colin who'd have to pull with her next. It was highly likely given the long-haul flight needed to get to her end of the table she'd be pulling her own cracker.

Noah donned his party hat and put the plastic car down to unfold the piece of paper that had fallen out along with the rest of his winnings.

'Shall I read your joke out, Noah.'

He inspected the paper and decided it was beyond his 'cat, sat on the mat' capacity because he got up and gave it to his mother.

'Why does Santa's sack bulge in every picture? Because he only comes once a year.' Roisin took a moment to digest what she'd just said before looking up to see a stunned Colin and Elsa staring down the table at her.

'I don't understand, Mummy. Everybody knows Santa only comes once a year. Why is it funny?'

'Erm...'

'It's not funny, Noah, not funny at all. Colin go and get the cracker box it's in the bin outside the back door.'

Colin looked reluctant but did as he was told as Noah continued to mutter about Santa's bulging sack.

'I didn't read it before I read it,' Roisin offered lamely.

'Mummy, did you not have your glasses on when your bought these because it says Adult Only up the top there,' Colin said, returning with the offending box.

Elsa spluttered that it was a disgrace such things were even on the market and that she would be writing a letter to her local paper about it. 'Christmas,' she sniffed was about family not pornographic Christmas cracker jokes.'

Roisin sipped her wine in order to swallow down the bubble of manic laughter that was threatening to float forth.

'What's pornographic? Noah asked, his eyes swinging from one to the other.

'Something you don't need to know about,' Elsa snapped. 'Right, Colin, put that down and sort the goose.'

Colin got on with carving and dishes were passed around before the serious business of eating began. Noah forgot all about geese and pornography in his horror at finding a Brussel sprout on his plate. 'It's a baby cabbage, Noah, it won't poison you,' Roisin explained. 'They're very good for you.'

'You said baby cabbages make Daddy's blow-offs really stinky.'

Roisin stopped, fork midway to her mouth, her pinching toe itching to give her son a jolly good nudge under the table as Colin and Elsa glared down at her.

Elsa changed the subject. 'More goose, Roisin, you can manage more than a wing surely,' she asked as Roisin popped the potato she'd speared in her mouth and tried to get rid of the taste of the rich meat.

'Oh, no, I couldn't fit anything else in, thanks, Elsa. It's all so delicious.' She laid her knife and fork down and waited for the others to do the same. The lone sprout rolled around on her son's plate but she didn't have the energy to encourage him to eat it so, getting up she announced she'd clear the table, managing to spirit it away before Elsa noticed.

'You go and sit down.' Elsa appeared in the kitchen behind her. 'While I sort the brandy butter for the pudding.'

Roisin mustered up a smile and left quick smart, having no desire to be alone with the older woman. She wandered back to the dining room where Noah was playing with his plastic car and Colin, who'd set out fresh glasses, was filling them with a sweet dessert wine. The air was heavy with the memory of all the food they'd just consumed. How strange it was to feel like she was in the room with a stranger but as she looked at Colin that was exactly how she felt. She could sense his underlying animosity at the situation they were now in as he put the wine down on the table and sat back down to stare into his glass. They were both struggling with how they were supposed to be around one another. The idea of chit-chat seemed like such a lot of hard work. Divorce had not been on Colin's agenda but then neither had losing their home. She'd have felt sorry for him if he hadn't hidden the whole sorry mess from her. He'd gone behind her back re-mortgaging their home, not bothering to consult her in his arrogant certainty his business gambles would pay off.

She'd wondered more than once *when* he would have bothered informing her that he'd lost everything or whether he'd been planning to leave it up to the bailiffs to let her know. One thing she did know was she wouldn't have lasted five minutes under Elsa's roof while he toiled away at getting back on his feet. He would too, men like Colin always did. He was a mover and a shaker, he knew people, and he'd climb back up his corporate ladder. He'd get over their marriage break-up too. They weren't and never had been a well-suited couple and his shonky business deal had merely been the catalyst not the cause of their going their separate ways.

She took a sip of the wine, which was too sweet for her liking, and watched him from under her lashes. She wondered if he'd already met someone else. She examined that thought. It wasn't him moving on with another woman that bothered her, good luck to whoever filled her boots. What did bother her was whether that woman would be kind to her son. The way Colin operated he'd probably be engaged by the time she got wind of him having someone on the scene. Ah well, she'd cross that bridge when she came to it. Shay sprang to mind.

Shay with his slightly too long hair and lanky laidback demeanour. Oh, and the way he handled that fiddle of his. She'd met him on her last trip home and the timing couldn't have been worse. They'd only talked twice, the first time being at Aisling's other half's restaurant, Quinn's. He'd been playing the fiddle in the band and she'd literally locked eyes with him across the crowded room. They'd gone for a coffee too, just before she left Dublin, and aware of her messy situation he'd asked if ever he was in London, perhaps he could look her up. She'd taken his number and given him hers but she'd not heard a word since and she didn't have the nerve to call him.

There'd been an attraction between them that she'd never felt with Colin. Would she see him when she was back in Dublin? Her insides quivered at the thought of him. And then she had the same discussion she'd had with herself every time she'd thought about Shay since she'd returned to London.

You're too old for him, Roisin. Sure, cop on to yourself, you're not in your twenties anymore you're nudging the dark side of your thirties and you're carrying cargo-sized emotional baggage. No man wants to sign on for that.

I'm not that old, thank you very much, and nobody would think twice about a man going out with a woman a few years younger than him. Why is it always different when the tables are turned?

How should I know? It just is and it's more than a few years.

Jaysus, I'm not after wanting to marry the fella, but a ride would be nice.

Yes, I'd have to agree with you on that one.

The dialogue usually closed there and a vivid scene in which she was riding Shay triumphantly toward the finish line would play out. It was the best bit but there was to be no imaginary riding today, not with the Christmas pudding having just arrived.

Elsa was carrying the dish as though it were the royal crown being brought to her Majesty. Noah's plastic car was forgotten and he was sitting up very straight in his chair staring eagerly at the steaming podgy dome as it was placed with reverence on the table. He was keen to sink his teeth into it because Granny had told him there were five-pence pieces hidden in it. Just so long as he didn't break a tooth or the like chomping into it, Roisin thought, catching a whiff of whisky and brandy butter. Jaysus, he'd be pie-eyed by the time he'd finished. Elsa doled the boozy pud out and Roisin debated whether she should suggest Noah might be better off with a bowl of ice cream. There'd be no money hidden in that though and it was only a small portion Elsa was giving him, so she decided to stay mute. Well, almost.

'Noah, chew carefully,' she warned as he tucked in. A moment later he gave an ecstatic cry and made a show of spitting the pudding out before poking his tongue out to show everyone the foil wrapped money.

'Okay, son, that's enough now.' Colin finally decided to parent as Noah did his best Gene Simmons impersonation before taking the money off his tongue and putting it down on the table.

Roisin eyed Elsa, who'd also found treasure and then Colin, who grimaced as his teeth clamped on something solid. She rifled through her pudding with her spoon but there was nothing in it other than fruit. The old bat had probably rigged it that way, she thought, stuffing the rest of it down her, knowing she was going to feel queasy later when the gamey meat and brandy butter decided to rendezvous in her stomach.

The clatter of spoons ceased and Roisin got up, keen to disappear into the kitchen for a bit of peace. Between Noah's monologue about how much he'd love a gerbil for Christmas and Elsa's chatter about how the council were letting the bin men away with murder, and Colin going on about a new deal her head was beginning to hurt. 'I'm on dishes, Elsa. It's only fair, you did all the hard work cooking.' She didn't receive any argument and she left them to retire to the front room once more to let their lunch go down and hopefully let Noah rip into a few of the packages under the tree. She set about clearing the table, carrying them through to the kitchen and stacking them on the worktop. She felt rather Cinderella-like as she rolled her sleeves up and plunged her hands into a sink full of sudsy water.

What was it Mammy used to say to them when they'd moan and groan over their chores? Roisin pondered, wiping down the worktop once she'd finally finished. 'You girls are making a mountain out of a molehill. Jaysus, Mary and Joseph if you spent as much time doing the dishes as you do moaning about being asked to get off your arses you'd have been back giving yourself the square eyes in front of that idiot box by now.' It made her smile. Well, Mammy, you'd be proud of me now, she thought casting her eyes around the sparkling kitchen. Elsa would have no cause for complaint either, it was shipshape. As she hung the tea towel over the oven door, she heard a squeal. It was a good squeal, an excited one and she was keen to see what had prompted it. In just over two hours she'd be on her way home; the thought put a spring in her step as she ventured back to the warmth of the front room.

Her son was sitting with his back to the door she saw pushing it open, and wrapping paper was strewn every which way. Noah heard her come in and swung his head around, his face lit up like the fairy lights on the tree. She'd put money on it not being a new dressing gown or bubble bath that had him grinning from ear to ear.

'Look, Mummy, look. This is the best Christmas ever!'

'What is it?' She smiled, his enthusiasm infectious as she glanced over at Elsa and Colin who were both perched on the edge of the Ercol sofa looking smug. The chinless gene had clearly been passed down from mother to son but had, mercifully, bypassed her handsome little lad. She turned her attention back to Noah who was swivelling round on his bottom dragging something along for the ride.

'Mummy,' he announced proudly, 'come and meet Mr Nibbles.'

Jaysus, feck! Roisin jumped as something made a scuttling sound. She was looking at a cage, she registered. A cage in which a chubby, brown and white gerbil was happily rifling through the torn paper scattered over the bottom of it. She blinked just to make sure she wasn't imagining things but no, the fat little mammal was showing off now doing a circuit on its wheel. Anger pricked through the surprise like a pin popping balloons. How dare Colin buy their son his first pet without checking in with her. She was going to be fun mammy, the mammy who bought her son a gerbil for Christmas. She conveniently pushed aside the little voice that said, "no you weren't". The point was she might have and now that choice had been snatched from her. Why hadn't he asked her how she felt about Noah getting a gerbil? Roisin knew the answer to that question. He hadn't asked because Colin never did. Colin did what he wanted to do. She was and always had been an irrelevant member of their family. She pivoted exorcist style to glare at him.

'It would have been nice if you'd talked to me about—'

'Mr Nibbles,' her big eared son piped up.

'Mr Nibbles.' The name came out sounding clipped and sharp.

'Well, you've been hard to get hold of now that you're working full time and he's talked about nothing else since November. I didn't think you'd mind, knowing how much he had his heart set on it.' Colin looked so pleased with himself her poor pinched toes burned with the urge to put the boot in, hard.

'You're not mad are you, Mummy?'

Roisin realised she had a choice here. She could be mean Mammy who wouldn't let her son have his heart's desire, a pet gerbil, for Christmas. Not a lot to ask for in the scheme of things, or she could embrace the fact she would be sharing her home from now on with Mr Nibbles. Colin had already pipped her at the post present wise and the thought of that saw her lips force themselves into a smile. 'Of course not, sweetheart. It's just that we're going on the aeroplane to Dublin tomorrow. I think Daddy might have forgotten about that because we won't be able to take Mr Nibbles with us. The airline won't let us, Noah.'

Noah's bottom lip jutted out and began trembling.

'Daddy didn't forget, Roisin, I rang the airline and checked and Mr Nibbles can travel as checked baggage so long as he has the proper cage, which he does. So, there's no problem.'

'There's no problem, Mummy,' Noah echoed.

'Ah, but it would be very traumatic for him.' Roisin did not want to take Mr Nibbles to Dublin. What if the little fecker had a heart attack mid-air? Noah would be beside himself and Christmas would be ruined. Besides, Mammy had a thing about small furry things ever since she'd had that encounter with a bold mouse who'd tickled her hair when she was sleeping. She'd thought their daddy was being friendly in the middle of the night and it was only when she realised he was snoring his head off that it couldn't have been him playing with her hair, and if it wasn't him then who was it? All hell had let loose, she'd charged around the apartment with the vacuum cleaner hose in the wee hours trying to get it and swearing she'd not sleep another wink ever again until she had proof he was gone. She and Aisling had thought it hilarious and tormented her something wicked by leaving a cat's toy mouse out in the most unexpected of places. No, Mammy couldn't be doing with a gerbil.

'He only has a teeny-tiny heart, Noah, and going on a big plane would be very frightening.'

'My friend, Marjorie, from the Knitters who Natter, travels with her Chihuahua, Petal, over to Ireland all the time, her daughter's over there.' Elsa joined in on the great Mr Nibbles debate waving her hand dismissively. 'Petal loves air travel.'

'Yes, but a chihuahua and a gerbil are two very different things,' Roisin pointed out, not quite believing she was having this discussion.

'Well,' Colin said, and there was something about the way in which he looked like he was playing poker and was about to lay down a royal flush that put Roisin on high alert. 'You can't expect Noah to be parted from Mr Nibbles when he's only just got him, Roisin, and if you're really not happy about him flying then Noah and the gerbil could always stay here with me and Mummy for the week.'

Arse! He had her over a barrel.

'Mummy?' Noah looked uncertain, torn between wanting to be with Mr Nibbles and the thought of not being with his mummy and seeing his other nana, and Aunty Aisling and Aunty Moira.

'Ah, well now, I'm sure he'll be fine but, Noah, he's your responsibility. That's what having a pet is all about.'

Noah nodded and began telling Mr Nibbles all about the Irish side of the family he would meet tomorrow.

'Right, that's settled. A lot of unnecessary fuss about nothing, I say.' Elsa sniffed. 'Now, who's for a game of charades?'

Chapter 5

Dublin's Arrivals hall was a shifting mass of bodies. Several planes had landed and disgorged their passengers simultaneously and Roisin told Noah to stay by her side as she grabbed an empty trolley. She was sorely tempted to ram a few pushy, shovey types in the back of the legs with it as she navigated their way through their fellow travellers, most of whom didn't seem to be filled with the Christmas spirit just yet. Air travel could do that to a person, Roisin mused, looking for their carousel. 'That's us over there, come on, Noah. Here hop on.' Noah balanced on the trolley and she wheeled in close to the conveyer belt to wait for the bags and one very special gerbil to begin trundling around.

'Mummy.' Noah clambered off the trolley and tugged at her coat sleeve. 'Will Nana be back to normal or will she still have clown hair and a big cast on her foot?' He wanted to be prepared this time, Roisin realised as the carousel suddenly rumbled into life. Poor love had been disturbed by his Nana's Bo Derek braids and casty foot the last time he'd seen her. To be fair she hadn't looked much better once she'd had the braids unplaited either; she'd been left with a cloud of hair akin to Ronald McDonald's. Noah had been very standoffish with his imposter Nana and she'd had to resort to base line bribery in the form of chocolate and sweets to win him around.

'She's all back to normal,' Roisin reassured her son, leaning on the trolley, well as close to normal as Mammy was ever likely to get at any rate. The state of her hair and foot on their last visit was down to her having just arrived home from her mammy-daughter trip with Moira to Vietnam. The country was on Mammy's bucket list due to her desire to sail on a junk. They'd all thought she was mad when she announced she was going there and poor Moira had found herself roped in for the journey. As it happened the pair of them had a great time apart from an ill-fated hike which had resulted in Mammy's broken ankle, and as for the braids, well she'd had no excuse for that other than it had looked the part at the time.

Roisin shuddered at the memory of Mammy driving them all demented as she issued orders from the sofa with her big casty foot resting on the coffee table. She'd even had to help Mammy off the loo after she'd dropped her crutches. Scarred, she was, scarred she thought, shaking the visuals away. She'd only had a few weeks of it, but poor Aisling and Moira had been ready to send her back to Vietnam with a "do not return" sticker by the time she finally got the plaster off and could go home to fend for herself. The first of the cases bounced past, a welcome distraction, and Noah pushed ahead to peer around the legs of a man in a suit trying to see if there was any sign of Mr Nibbles.

'Do you think he'll be alright, Mummy?' he tossed back over his shoulder.

'Yes, bound to be.' Roisin had prayed the entire flight that he would be.

'He's coming, Mummy!' Noah jiggled up and down on the spot, knocking suit man who gave him the kind of look that was alright for a mammy and daddy to give their child but not for a stranger and Roisin resisted the urge to trolley ram once more. Self-important eejit she muttered to herself as she too spied the handle of the cage just visible above the rucksack currently doing the rounds. She eyed her son, recognising the jiggle. She'd been caught out on many occasions by it, usually when they were miles from any sort of a convenience. 'Do you need a wee-wee before we leave the airport? Because now's the time to say if you do, Noah, not when we're halfway to your nana's and there's nowhere to go.'

'No, I don't, I just want Mr Nibbles.' He pushed forward again receiving another look and she took action yanking him back. 'It's rude to push in. Let me get him off and then you can be in charge of him.'

The cage trundled closer and she readied herself sending up a quick prayer that the gerbil be alive and well before sidling in alongside the suit man, giving him an accidental shove on purpose before hoisting the cage off. She handed it to her son who took it from her reverently. 'I can see our case, wait a sec, once I've got it, we'll move out the way and you can check on Mr Nibbles,' she instructed.

How was it the case felt heavier heaving it off the conveyer than it had when she'd heaved it on the weighing scale at Heathrow? One of life's mysteries, Roisin decided, moving away from the throng still waiting to retrieve their luggage. She came to a standstill. 'Alright, Noah, let's see how he's doing.' She watched, breath held, as he set the cage down before carefully removing the cover. She exhaled as a pair of unblinking eyes stared up at them, a piece of lettuce clutched between two teeny front paws. She'd half expected to find the gerbil flat on his back, tiny legs rigid in the air and the relief of it all made her want to track down the Aer Lingus pilot and thank him for being such a good pilot and giving them a smooth flight.

Noah was inspecting the cage. 'He's done lots of poo, Mummy.'

'Ah well now, he's regular that's all. It's down to all those greens you've been feeding him. Plenty of roughage, like I'm always after telling you.'

'But I don't want to poo all the time. That's why I don't eat my broccoli.'

Ah the way a five-year-old's brain worked was a wondrous thing indeed, Roisin thought, debating whether to spiel off her broccoli is a superfood speech but then she remembered where she was and who would be doing a jiggle dance akin to Noah's if they didn't get a move on. 'C'mon with you, Nana will be waiting.' He picked up the cage once more and they trundled over to join the end of the snaking line filing through customs. It was moving swiftly which meant everybody was behaving themselves today, apart from the family of four who were now at the front of the queue. The mammy and the daddy were arguing over the organisation of their cases on the trolley which were tottering like a Jenga stack as they moved forward. They stood out, thanks to their tomato glow, and Roisin knew if Mammy were with her, she'd rush on up and tell them to get themselves a tube of the E45 cream. She wouldn't be able to help herself because just as the Bible was to the Christian, the E45 cream was to Mammy when it came to the first sign of anyone's skin erupting in anything red. She'd slathered them in the stuff if they'd caught too much sun or had any sort of a rash threating to make an appearance when they were small.

'Mummy, why's that man getting shouted at by that lady got mouse ears on? He looks silly.'

'I think they've been to Disneyland, Noah. You know where Mickey Mouse and Donald Duck live.' She didn't add and where eejits like yer man there who are old enough to know better come home with chronic sunburn and a pair of fecking mouse ears perched on his head. Impatience was making her snarky and she practised her breathing until at last the Mouseketeer family were waved through and the line began to shorten once more. Finally, it was their turn.

'Mummy, should we have got Mr Nibbles a passport?' Noah asked as they approached the booth.

'No, son, he's grand.' She smiled at the customs man expecting him to smile back indulgently at her boy's sweet concern for his pet. He didn't. He was all business as he took the burgundy booklets from her while Noah held the cage up proudly to show him. He was too busy scrutinising Roisin's dodgy passport photo to notice Noah jiggling away desperate to get a look in. A frown Roisin fancied as one of suspicion was embedded between a pair of brows that for some reason made her think of Brooke Shields back in the day and thinking of Brooke Shields made her think of Mammy, not that there was any resemblance whatsoever but because as a teenager she'd been desperate to see *The Blue Lagoon*. Mammy had forbidden her from going even though she'd been fifteen nearly sixteen at the time. 'It's for your own good, Roisin, you'd only have to tell Father Fitzpatrick that you're after going to see a pornographic film in the confession. Kate Finnegan says there's boobies and yer man Christopher you're so keen on flashes his winky, a lot.' Roisin hadn't though that telling her mammy that was why she wanted to see the film would sway the odds in her favour. She never had gotten to see Christopher Atkins' winky, she lamented now as Mr Customs, who she saw upon inspection was called Declan, eyed her before returning to his passport scrutiny. She could hear someone cough and imagined a great deal of impatient shuffling going on in the queue behind them.

'Is something the matter, Declan?' Yes, it was bold of her being on first name terms with a man who had the power to stop her entering her own country but sure they were all Irish, weren't they? He didn't look up and she began to feel guilty. Of what, she wasn't sure but a sweat broke out on her forehead further incriminating her, nonetheless. Okay, so she'd blinked and the half-opened eyes she was sporting in the picture he was studying along with lank hair she should have washed before getting the photo taken but had been in too much of a big, disorganised rush to do so wasn't the best. She'd hold her hand up to understanding that she had the look of someone who might have a kilo of the hard stuff strapped to their person in it but, all he had to do was look at her face to see she'd struggle to smuggle in so much as an extra carton of cigarettes, if she smoked that was. The seconds ticked by with him not answering her and just as she was about to throw herself on his mercy and shout, 'I'm innocent!' He snapped her passport shut and slid them both back to her. Noah seized his chance.

'This is Mr Nibbles, my gerbil, I only got him yesterday he's coming with me and Mum to stay with Nana and my aunties for Christmas.'

At last Declan turned his attention to the jiggling lad. 'Ah well now, I'm sure they'll be looking forward to meeting yer man there.' He leaned down from his perch and peered into the cage. 'Hello there, Mr Nibbles, did you have a good flight?'

Roisin wondered if he'd get through the rest of his shift without the two buttons stretched over his middle pinging off and Jaysus, now that she looked properly, the poor man had a nasty case of razor burn going on there, so he did. She was pleased Mammy was on the other side of the wall because if she saw the state of his neck, she'd be recommending the E45 cream to him too.

'It was his first time on an aeroplane and he's gone and done a lot of poo,' Noah explained earnestly. 'Mummy says it's because of all the greens he eats which is why I don't eat my broccoli but I think he was scared of being up in the sky.'

Declan looked a little taken aback at the turn the conversation had taken. It wasn't every day he encountered a little boy with a broccoli aversion whose mother looked like a hardened drug smuggler in her passport photo along with a gerbil that had shat himself because he was frightened of flying.

'Ah well then, best you get on your way to your nana's house so you can sort the poor fella out. A Merry Christmas to you both.' He waved them through and Roisin heard a smattering of applause behind her. She didn't look back as she said, 'And to you,' before heading for the sliding doors of freedom.

Mammy had informed Roisin over the telephone when they'd gotten home yesterday that she would wear a bright yellow sweater and black chinos so as to be easily identifiable. Her tone had been hushed as though she were a spy in the cold war. Indeed, she'd told Roisin she'd seen a very good film the night before called *From Russia with Love*. She was always very easily influenced, was Mammy.

'But, Mammy,' Roisin had said. 'It's Dublin airport, it's not exactly JFK. I'll be able to find you.'

'It's busy this time of the year, Rosi. You'll thank me for it. Yellow sweater, remember that, and you'll be grand.'

'Look for a yellow sweater, Noah.'

'There, Mum, over there.'

She followed the line of her son's finger and spotted her mammy jumping up and down waving out. She was a busy bee with swishy dark hair in a garden of weary travellers, Roisin thought poetically. Mammy was right she was grateful for her sunny colour scheme. She always felt sorry for people who walked through those doors and had no one waiting to greet them. Although, she thought waving back, she'd want to stop with the star jumps or she'd likely have an accident.

Noah rushed on ahead keen to introduce the newest member of the family. The cage was banging against his leg and Roisin called out for him to slow down even though she knew she was wasting her breath. Poor Mr Nibbles was really being put through the wringer today and once again, she cursed Colin. What had he been thinking? She slowed her pace. It was Noah who'd been adamant that Mr Nibbles was coming to Dublin so, let him explain to his nana why he had a furry friend in tow.

Dragging her heels, she witnessed fear followed by horror flashing in her mammy's eyes as she looked at the cage and shrieked, 'Jesus, Mary and Joseph, Noah, what's that?' She looked up then seeking out her daughter and pinned her down with a set of twin tasers. 'Roisin Quealey nee O'Mara, get yourself over here now.'

Charming, what happened to welcome home, darling? Her mammy's stinger was definitely out, Roisin thought, knowing there was nowhere to run to. She pulled up alongside her son.

'Did you know about this?' Maureen O'Mara, her face a mottled red, jabbed in the direction of the cage.

'Erm that Noah was bringing Mr Nibbles on holiday?'

'Don't be clever with me, young lady, it doesn't suit you. You know what I'm talking about. The rat your son has got in that cage. You do know the plague was started by rats, don't you? Dirty, filthy, vermin.' She shivered for effect.

'Nana!' Noah was aghast. 'Mr Nibbles isn't a rat, he's a gerbil and he's very nice. Look,' he held the cage up as high as he could and Maureen jumped back with a shriek.

'Get it away from me!'

'Mammy get a grip of yourself,' Roisin hissed, embarrassed by the stares they were garnering. 'It's a gerbil like Noah said. He can't hurt you.'

'It's small and furry with big teeth, what's the difference?'

'He's a mammal, not a rodent,' Roisin said. She'd looked it up knowing the information would come in handy but she hadn't expected to have to drop it in before they'd even left the airport.

'Well, I'm not going to be responsible for Pooh. He might think your gerbil rat there is a new toy.' Pooh was Maureen's poodle. It was down to Roisin she had a dog as the last time she'd been in Dublin a friend had been looking to rehome their puppy. Twins and a puppy had not been a good idea, her friend had cried down the telephone, and Roisin having heard her mammy making noises about getting a nice little doggy to keep her company had thought it a great idea for their poodle pup to come and live with Mammy. She'd heard the word "poodle" and pictured a small, yappy little dog that would prance around her mammy's ankles and sit on her lap to watch *Fair City* of an evening. Only, it transpired Pooh wasn't a toy poodle he was a standard and was now four times the size he'd been when Roisin had last seen him. She knew Mammy had made concerted efforts to change the pups name from Pooh upon adoption but he would not answer to anything else and so it had stuck.

'He'll be staying in his cage for the duration we're at yours. Won't he, Noah? Sure, it will be grand, Mammy, don't worry.'

'There she goes, Easy-osi, Rosi with her "she'll be grand" attitude.' Mammy shook her head and muttered things like dead gerbil and what was that daughter of hers thinking bringing it to Dublin, all the way out to the car.

They'd only just pulled out into the steady traffic when Noah tapped Roisin on the shoulder.

'I need a wee-wee, Mum.'

Chapter 6

Roisin was nearly knocked to the ground by a yapping blur of woolly black curls as she followed Mammy into her apartment. Noah shot off for the toilet leaving Mr Nibbles on his nana's dining table and her to fend off Pooh who had a paw resting either side of the top of her legs. She could smell his hot panting, doggy breath as he gazed up at her before trying to bury his head in her nether regions. 'Mammy, get him off me!'

'Down, boy,' Maureen said, giving him a tap.

Pooh ignored her. She looked at her daughter. 'He likes you, Rosi. He has a thing for the ladies so he does. Rosemary Farrell won't visit me at home anymore unless I promise to put him in the spare room and you want to hear the fuss he makes when he thinks he's missing out.' Maureen got him by the collar and dragged him off her. 'You're a very naughty boy, Poosy-woosy, aren't you?' She gave him a pat on the head just to really hammer her point home, and a bit of a cuddle before looking at Roisin who was sidling through the apartment with her case positioned in front of her in case he came back for round two.

'You never spoke to us like that when we were naughty, Mammy,' she shot back. 'And you certainly didn't give us a pat on the head. The wooden spoon on our backside was what we got.' She was a bit put out by the amount of attention the poodle was receiving. She wondered how Moira was coping having had her position as the baby of the family, one she revelled in, usurped.

'You only got the wooden spoon when you were bold and I've enrolled Pooh in puppy obedience school. He starts in the new year.' She looked at the poodle and then back at Roisin, lowering her voice to a barely audible whisper. 'He's getting his you know what's seen to as well in January. It's for his own good but he won't see it that way, I mean, would you? The vet's after telling me it will help with aggressive behaviour as he gets older and marking his territory that sorta thing. He won't get nasties down there either like the cancer. I'm hoping it will help with this habit of going around putting his nose in places it has no business going too because it's getting out of hand and it's embarrassing so it is. The rambling girls are beginning to talk thanks to Rosemary.'

'We can't have that now, can we?' Roisin whispered back, and Maureen shot her a look, unsure whether she was being clever or not.

She dared move her gaze from the poodle to the artwork on the wall. Moira's painting of Foxy-Loxy had won her first place in a well-respected children's art competition when she was a child. It was nice to see the familiar painting hanging on a wall in a room that otherwise felt strangely out of kilter to her. The apartment opened up into the living room, the kitchen was at the far end and to the right of the open plan space a utility room was tucked away off the kitchen. Over to Roisin's left was the door that led to the hall where two generous bedrooms were positioned opposite each other. A large picture window was the living room's focal point. On a clear day it afforded a glimpse of blue from the sea but today she could see the rain spattered glass and knew the view would be murky. She'd grown used to an urban outlook, Roisin realised, and the presence of a yipping poodle her mammy was infatuated with was only exacerbating the feeling of being somewhere new and foreign instead of in her mammy's home. She'd get used to it she supposed.

Actually, now that she was taking a moment to look around, she realised the living room had a Vietnamese village feel to it. Or, at least how she imagined a Vietnamese village would feel. Although the village houses probably didn't have sofas and big tellies in them. She smiled recalling the postcard Moira had sent to Noah that made mention of their mammy having gotten very excited over the local village's handicrafts and she'd been worried she was going to get herself a Joseph and his Technicoloured coat in the local brocade fabric. She'd contented herself with cushion covers and throw blankets instead which were now strewn artfully around the sofa and chairs. Vibrant hues of striped, pink, purple and oranges adding pops of colour to an otherwise neutral décor. Her eyes flitted about the space noting the high gloss, brilliant red, purple and blue lacquerware she'd managed to get home in one piece, on display on the built-in wall shelves. She bit back a laugh seeing the erect, wooden fertility symbol, Mammy had carved on her trip and which she was adamant was in fact a canoe. A row of Christmas cards stood to attention on the next shelf and on the top shelf was the infamous conical hat Moira had been unable to stop her from wearing during their trip. It had feet poking out from under it, she realised frowning, and she could see a tulle skirt too.

Mammy followed her gaze. That's Annabel under there. I never could stand her but I always think if I put her away, your great granny will strike me down with lightening. That, I feel, is a good compromise.'

Roisin agreed. She'd never liked the china doll heirloom either. It had always felt like she was watching them all, following them about with those icy blue eyes from wherever it was she was perched.

'Oh, you've a tree!' It was positioned in the smaller window beside the dining table, a fake one but a definite cut above Roisin's Argos special. It had twinkly fairy lights strewn around its tinsel branches and decorations she knew she'd recognise from when she was a child were she to take a closer look.

'I don't know why you sound so surprised. Just because I'm on my own, with the exception of Pooh, doesn't mean I should let my standards drop and besides it gives the neighbour across the way something to look at. Nosy old bint she is.'

Roisin peered out the window behind the tree half expecting to see a disgruntled old woman peering back at her.

'Go on and put your bag in your room. You can hang your coats up in the utility room. I'll put the kettle on. I think we'll have a nice cup of tea and a slice of Christmas cake. It's a lovely moist one this year.'

Roisin's mouth watered at the thought of a nice big slab of Mammy's fruit cake. Noah wouldn't like the cake with its boozy, fruity, spiced flavour but he'd snaffle down the marzipan icing no problem.

'Then I thought we'd wrap up and take Pooh for a stroll along the pier. It might wear him out before dinner with your sisters tonight. Moira's threatening to do the you-know-what personally if he comes near her again.'

'He's not coming, is he?' Roisin had assumed she'd have a randy puppy-free evening ahead.

'Oh, I can't leave him on his own for long, Roisin, it wouldn't be fair. You wouldn't have liked it if I'd left you home alone when you were wee, now would you?'

Roisin shook her head. Pooh was clearly part of the family these days and it would seem he was laying claim to being the favoured child despite his dirty ways. If they weren't careful, he'd be the one Mammy would leave her worldly goods to. She nearly collided with Noah who'd finished his business. 'Did you wash your hands?'

'I need to say hello to Pooh.'

'Hands! Wait a sec and give me that coat.' Roisin tugged it off him. 'Now hands.'

He stomped back to the bathroom to complete the job while she hung their coats up on the hooks on the back of the small room off the kitchen. Then she walked back through the living room seeing Mammy was busying herself in the kitchen. She picked up her bag and carried it through to the bedroom. There was no hint of her mammy's recent trip in here she saw, looking about and noting that it was tastefully done, painted in a soft cream. Curtains in a deeper green framed a window that overlooked the charming street below and a black and white photograph of a lily took centre place on the wall above the bed. The bed looked inviting with its matching cream and green linen, the pillows she noticed, with a feeling of longing, were plumped to perfection. Roisin was tempted to lie down and rest her head on one just for a few minutes but she didn't dare leave Noah alone with Mr Nibbles and Pooh for long. Mammy never scrimped when it came to bedding and she knew how to fold corners better than any nurse who'd been trained in the art by a stern matron could.

Yes, she'd be very comfortable in here. Well, as comfortable as she could expect to be with her son in the bed next to her. Noah turned into a prize kickboxer in his sleep! She opened her case and hung a few things in the wardrobe that would be a crumpled wreck if she left them folded in her bag, before opening the door once more. She peeked around it to check Pooh was otherwise engaged and wouldn't be homing in for another full-frontal assault. He was sitting on his pillow being petted by Noah, all the while watching Mammy. She was laying the tea things out on the table and the puppy had a look of total adoration on his face. She warmed to him, it was nice to know Mammy was loved and looked after, even if it was by a frisky poodle.

'Mummy?' Noah got up spying his mother skulking back into the room. 'I need to change the newspaper for Mr Nibbles.' He turned his attention to his nana who was putting a few biscuits on a plate. 'He did lots of poo on the plane because he was frightened, Nana.'

Roisin had a horrible feeling her son had developed a fixation when it came to his gerbil's motions and that everyone as well as their uncle would have heard about Mr Nibble's way of demonstrating his fear of flying by the time the day was done. 'I told Pooh that he has to be kind to him too because that's what you have to do when someone's smaller and weaker than you and I don't want poor Mr Nibbles to do any more poo.'

He'd obviously been paying attention to the Stop Bullying talk his classroom had had the other week then, Roisin deduced. It was a pity he didn't have quite the same aptitude to listening when it came to the rest of his schoolwork.

'Neither do I, thanks very much, and Noah get him off my table.' Maureen gave the cage a push nudging it precariously close to the edge 'That's my best lace cloth you've got that filthy thing on.' She looked over at Roisin with her lips pursed disapprovingly and her eyes raked over her daughter, coming to a halt when they reached her pants. 'Those are nice. They look ever so comfy, especially around your middle.' She patted her own to emphasise her point.

'They're only yoga pants, Mammy. I've tons of pairs. I live in them when I'm not working.' Roisin looked down at the soft, black stretchy synthetic material. They had a folded over waistband that sat on her hips and the leg was bootcut. They were comfortable and her go-to most days. Her days of trying to play the corporate wife, and not very successfully at that, were done. There was a glint in her mammy's eyes that made her wary of the sudden interest in her pants. She did a quick count trying to remember how many pairs she'd brought with her so she'd know if any went missing. Three, she'd brought three with her. She knew her mammy had developed a penchant for slacks because Aisling and Moira had filled her in on the fisherman pants she was so fond of, although she'd yet to see them for herself. Moira had also been horrified by the amount she spent on a pair of travel trousers for their trip. Mammy's reasoning had been that she'd needed all the pockets her whizz bang, quick dry pants afforded her. Moira reckoned she was on a mission to burn through the family inheritance.

'Yoga pants you say. Well I never. Turn around and give us a look at the back.'

Against her better judgment, Roisin did as she was told.

'Oh, Roisin, they give your bottom ever such a lovely shape. It looks like a peach so it does. Have they secret lift properties in them?'

'My bum doesn't need any secret lifting, thank you.' She craned her neck over her shoulder trying to cop a look at her peach in case things had dropped since she'd last checked.

'Well, I think they must do because I know your backside as well as I know the back of my hand and it was never that perky. Do you think they'd do the same for mine?' Maureen was fixated with Roisin's rear.

'Jaysus, Mammy, listen to you and stop staring.' She turned around.

Mammy was unapologetic she had a one-track mind at times and this was one of those times. 'They're not just for the bendy yoga stuff, then? You can wear them just because they're super soft and stretchy but look smart at the same time.'

'Yes, I wear them all the time for casual.' Roisin was wearing a white top and had a denim jacket in her suitcase she liked to teem with it but today had been definite coat and scarf weather. She lived in trainers these days too, unlike her sisters who were far more likely to be found compensating for their height with ridiculously high heels. She'd given up the ghost, accepting the crick in her neck from looking up when speaking to those blessed with average height as her lot. Aisling in particular was obsessed with the stiletto and maintained she had no need of the gym because her legs got an intensive workout everyday thanks to her choice of footwear. Any chance she got she'd be flashing you her calves and saying, 'Sure just look at the muscle tone.'

'And you've tons of pairs you say?'

Roisin saw too late where this was headed.

'Then you won't mind letting your dear old mammy try a pair on, now will you?' She lifted her sweater and showed Roisin the roll of flesh spilling over the top of her black chinos. 'They're cutting me in half so they are.'

'Put it away, Mammy. You'll give Noah nightmares.'

'Nana, have you got some newspaper, please?' Noah was oblivious to his nana exposing herself.

'I'll be right with you once your mammy fetches her spare yoga pants for me.'

Roisin knew the look she was currently on the receiving end of. It was a look that said you scratch my back, I'll scratch yours. Or, in this case—you get me the pants and I won't kick up about the gerbil.

She went and got the pants.

Chapter 7

'You'll find the old newspapers in the bottom cupboard of the sideboard,' Maureen said, snatching the black pants off Roisin before she changed her mind. 'I'll just go and slide these on.'

'Play tug-o-war, more likely,' Roisin muttered, going to retrieve the paper. She squatted down and pulled a few sheets of the newsprint loose; the title of a book that had been reviewed jumped out at her and falling back on to her bum she sat cross-legged scanning what the reviewer had to say about it. It was called, 'When We Were Brave' by Cliona Whelan. The author had swapped journalism for novel writing after a long career which had seen her at the forefront of women breaking into the male dominated newspaper world in Ireland back in the seventies. This was her first book, Roisin read, her attention well and truly caught. The actual review was all very high faluting and could have been summed up simply by saying *this was a great book, I recommend you read it.* They were a pretentious lot, those literary types. It *did* sound like a good story though, she thought, getting up. It would make a good Christmas present for Aisling; she was a reader. The thought of hitting the shops this time of year filled her with dread. It would be chaos but it had seemed silly to lug gifts over from London. She'd take Moira with her, she decided. Moira was good at getting people to move out of the way.

'Mummy,' Noah whined, growing ever more impatient, although she saw looking over, he had removed Mr Nibbles from the table. He'd set him down on the floor and was impatient to get on with the task at hand. For Pooh's part he seemed totally uninterested in the little creature but then, Roisin supposed that was probably because Mr Nibbles was a boy gerbil. That didn't mean she trusted him though.

'Come on then, we'll go in the bedroom to clean it all up.'

'Oh, no you don't. You can forget about cleaning that thing inside. Outside with the pair of you.' Maureen appeared in the living room doorway and gestured to her little balcony. A Parisian style table and chair looked forlorn as they were lashed by the wind and intermittent drizzle.

Roisin could almost hear the wind whistling from where she was standing. 'But, Mammy, it's freezing, the cold would kill him and what if he escapes?'

'Well you should have thought of that shouldn't you when you decided to bring that thing with you.'

'Nana, you're hurting his feelings and you're making me feel very sad.'

Another part of the Stop Bullying talk had been about how the children needed to express how they felt. Noah excelled at it and he wasn't finished yet either.

'I think you should say sorry to Mr Nibbles, Nana, or I'm going to cry. And, if he ran away or died because he was too cold, I'd be very, very, very, VERY sad.'

Maureen muttered a barely audible, 'Mr Nibbles my arse.'

'Mammy, don't be so mean.' Roisin added her pennies' worth and got straight to the point. 'And come on with you, let's see the pants.'

Maureen brightened instantly, flashing a big smile as she did her version of a model strutting down the catwalk coming to a halt in the middle of the living room, hands on hips, looking pleased with herself as she struck a pose. 'I got into them.'

'I can see that, Mammy.' Squeezed into them was more to the point. 'They don't leave much to the imagination.'

'They're grand, look...' she swung forward bending from her middle, her hair a curtain over her face as she tried to touch her toes and her voice was muffled as she said, 'I can even do the bendy yoga.'

Pooh tripped over himself in his excitement to get out of his basket.

'I'd watch out if I were you, Mammy.'

She righted herself quick smart, her face red and mottled with the exertion of it all. 'Don't you go getting any ideas.' She shook her finger at the poodle who skulked back to his basket.

'I might need to wear one of those e-strings under them you girls get about in.'

Roisin must have looked horrified at the thought because Maureen puffed up, 'Just because I'm a woman of certain years it doesn't mean I can't move with the times, Roisin.'

'To be fair, Mammy. I'm surprised you can move in them at all and I think you mean G-string.' She narrowed her eyes. She hadn't counted how many pairs of smalls she'd packed. 'You better not have—'

'As if I would.'

Noah interrupted, 'Nana, you still haven't said sorry.' He tapped his foot.

Maureen chewed her lip, her reluctance to grovel to a gerbil plain for all to see.

He raised an expectant eyebrow and Roisin choked back a laugh when he said, 'I haven't got all day you know.' He was parodying her giving him a telling off without even realising it.

Maureen saw the funny side of things and decided to go with it. 'I'm sorry I hurt your feelings, Mr Nibbles.'

'Mr Nibbles accepts your apology. There now that wasn't so bad was it. We'll say no more about it.'

'He's been here before,' Maureen said to Roisin. 'I'm sure of it.' She sighed. 'Let me keep the pants and you can use the utility room to clean his cage out.'

Roisin pulled her son in the direction of the tiny laundry space before she could change her mind. She didn't want the pants back now anyway. Not now that Mammy had stretched them.

THE AIR WAS BRACING enough to make Roisin's eyes water and a battering of stout rain drops were stinging her face. They'd enjoyed a cup of tea and a biscuit and then Mammy had made them rug up like snowmen to take Pooh for his afternoon walk. She was still in the yoga pants. 'Mammy, slow down,' she called, but her voice was lost on the salty air. She was holding Noah's hand tightly as they strode out along the pier. Maureen was grasping Pooh's leash with a grim determination, the poodle having set off down the long expanse of concrete jutting out to sea at an excitable clip. He was enjoying the briskness of his afternoon outing, his nose snuffling along smelling goodness knows what. Waves crashed either side of them and moored fishing boats bobbed in the frothing waters.

Roisin had images of her mammy getting airborne if her little legs were to pump any faster. She'd be like a red balloon floating away in that rain jacket of hers, she thought. Noah, wrapped up in his new coat, was holding the plastic bag eagerly awaiting the moment he could use the title his nana had bestowed on him of official pooper scooper. So far so good, all they'd been privy to were numerous incidents of lamppost leg cocking on the walk here. At last Pooh slowed to check out something unidentifiable and Roisin and Noah caught up to Maureen.

Maureen pointed at the yacht club and shouted over the wind. 'The Christmas dinner was last Saturday. I wore the red Vietnamese dress. You know the one Moira borrowed the night the three of you went to Quinn's for dinner in the matching dresses I had made especially for you in Hoi An. Everybody said it looked very well on me. I had a grand time. There was dancing and everything.'

How could she forget? It was the night she'd met Shay and who would have thought that the Chinese style silk dresses would have such an impact but Aisling's Quinn had barely been able to keep his hands to himself. Mind he struggled to at the best of times. As Moira was to Tom's superbly sculpted glutes, so was Quinn to Aisling's womanly rear. Tom had been rather taken with Moira in Mammy's red number even if it had hung off her in the places it would have had a stranglehold on Mammy. As for Shay, she didn't know what he'd thought about her enforced choice of evening wear but she did know there'd been a connection between them. Would she see him while she was here, or wouldn't she? Did she leave it to fate or did she call him?

'You've a daft look on your face.' Maureen peered at her daughter from under the hood of her raincoat.

'I haven't.'

'You have. Roisin, I've raised three daughters and I know that look. You've a man on your mind so you have.'

Roisin glanced guiltily at her son but he too was engaged in examining whatever the unspeakable thing Pooh was so interested in was and out of earshot. He'd adjusted to his new living arrangement but a new man on the scene was a different thing entirely, it was far too early to introduce anyone else into his life. Come to that she was getting so far ahead of herself where Shay was concerned it was ridiculous. Mammy read her mind.

'Is it yer man, Shay? You know, the grandson of the auld fella Noah was after tormenting the last time you were over.'

Noah had enjoyed a rambunctious game of knock on the door and run away with Reggie, Shay's estranged grandfather who'd been staying in Room 1 at O'Maras. The story had a happy ending, not for Noah—he'd had to apologise, but for Shay and his granddad who'd met for the first time. It was a new beginning before the end, because Reggie was terminally ill, but at least they'd had the chance to connect and get to know one another. She wondered how they were getting on, how Reggie was. He'd been a cantankerous old sod, made bitter by life but she'd seen past that and had liked him. She'd liked his grandson more but that was beside the point.

Roisin didn't say anything but Mammy looked jubilant as she prodded her in the chest. 'A-ha. It is. Moira was after telling me you were panting after him at Quinn's. I wasn't sure if it was just Moira making something out of nothing what with you and Colin only just having parted ways. But,' she jabbed at her again, 'I can tell by the way you look shifty. You had that same look on your face when you told me you'd found a job in the entertainment industry.'

'I had, though.' Roisin had lost count of how many times she'd protested this particular point.

'Roisin, wearing next to nothing and prancing your way around the city's nightspots while handing out free alcopops is not working in the entertainment industry.'

'Mammy, you make it sound seedy and it wasn't a bit like that. It was all about being entertaining as we promoted the product and the product happened to be sold in nightclubs.' Actually, it was quite a lot like that but it was a long time ago now and sure look at her these days—a mammy and a secretary in an accountancy firm. You couldn't get more respectable than that.

'Hmm, you did far too much promoting of your product in my opinion.'

They were getting off track, and what were Noah and Pooh so fascinated by? She moved closer, deciding it looked like some sort of dead mollusc. She winced as Pooh licked it and made a note not to let him near her. It was time for a subject change.

'So, you had dinner with the boatie brigade, that's nice.'

Maureen had taken sailing lessons last summer and loved to tell people she was a member of the Howth Sailing Club. Though, Roisin thought, looking at the wistful look on her face as she gazed out at the churning water, to be fair Mammy had been very brave. She'd tackled life head on after their daddy died what with moving out of O'Mara's, joining any club that would have her, trying new things and going on an Asian adventure. It was her way of finding her way without her husband at her side. The need to tell her how she felt swelled up in her like the surging waters on either side of them.

'Mammy, I'm very proud of you. I know I haven't told you that before, but I am.'

Maureen looked startled. 'Where did that come from?'

Roisin shrugged. 'I don't know. It's true though.'

'Well, I'm proud of you too, Roisin.'

Roisin's eyes inexplicably filled. 'Are you?'

'Of course, I am.' Maureen spotted the telltale glistening in Roisin's eyes. 'Ah now, don't be silly, c'mere and have a cuddle.' Mammy pulled her into a damp embrace and Roisin sniffed. So much had happened this year, so many changes, but she'd survived just as Mammy had. She looked past her mammy's shoulder and her eyes widened at the sight of Pooh frolicking around a woman in a turquoise rain jacket. A camera was in her hand and on the breeze floated what she was guessing was a Scandi version of 'feck off with you'.

'Mammy?' Roisin pulled away from her. 'You'd best sort Pooh out.'

Maureen turned just in time to see her pampered pooch joyfully snuffling around the woman's backside.

'Pooh O'Mara, you cut that out right now you dirty boy!'

Jaysus wept, thought Roisin, he really was part of the family. She'd have to tell her sisters about this.

Chapter 8

Their luck was in because Mammy had sneaked into a parking spot right outside the guesthouse and as they piled out of the car, Roisin glanced up at the red brick Georgian manor house. When she was growing up it had simply been home. Not your average family home granted, but home nonetheless. It was only once she'd moved away to London that she'd truly begun to appreciate how magical O'Mara's was and how lucky she was to have such a slice of the city's history in her family. It was part of Noah's legacy, she mused, feeling oddly poetic.

Maureen led the way, or rather Pooh did, and Roisin followed herding Noah toward the panelled, blue front door. It was topped by the small windows and white arching crown so typical of the famous Dublin doors in their pocket of the city. An enticing glow emanated through the multiple paned windows next to the door, a welcoming signal to come on in on this cold afternoon. It afforded a glimpse of the spectacular, sparkly Christmas tree inside ensuring no passers-by would be left in doubt that the festive season was upon them.

The tree was a focal point as soon as you stepped through the door. It was enormous, even bigger than Elsa's had been and Roisin hoped no tour groups were due to arrive while it stood to attention as it took up a good portion of the foyer. They'd have to line up and wait their turn outside to check in! It was a tree that Father Christmas himself would be proud of she thought, eying it as she bundled in behind Mammy, Pooh and Noah. This seemed to be the natural order of things, that Pooh was by Mammy's side. She'd been affronted that she'd had to sit in the back of the car with Noah on the ride over while Pooh, got to sit up front. Mammy had said he thought of it as his seat and it wouldn't be fair to change his routine. She could have sworn the poodle gave her a look that said, 'You better get used to it, sister, cos it's the way it's gonna be.'

She closed the door to the guesthouse quickly before the polar blast currently whistling down the pavement outside could follow them in. It was only four o'clock but the street lights outside were already on, their glow spilling pools of light onto the damp puddles. A steady stream of homeward bound traffic trickled past the Green.

Noah's eyes were out like organ stoppers and his mouth formed a delighted 'O' as he stared up at the tree, taking in all the gold blingy decorations dripping from it. Roisin spied his little hand reaching out, unable to resist touching the shiniest of the baubles. The woman responsible for putting this, the most glorious, or ridiculously oversized depending on how you looked at it, tree together, Bronagh, peered over the front desk to see what all the commotion was about. There were two bobbing reindeer on springs attached to the Alice band on her head. They danced about as she shot up from her seat to greet them only to be stopped dead in her tracks by Pooh. He charged for the receptionist, pinning her against the fax machine. She never stood a chance, Roisin thought, as her mammy gave her triceps yet another workout trying to rein him in. A kerfuffle ensued as she tugged him off her. 'Naughty boy, Pooh. A million apologies, Bronagh. He can't help himself. The tree looks fabulous—' Her voice was lost as he dragged her up the stairs.

Bronagh smoothed her rumpled cardigan and inspected her skirt for signs of muddy paw prints. Finding none she looked at Roisin and shook her head causing a frantic bobbing of the reindeer. 'Yer mam's gone soft in the head over that dog. I never thought I'd see the day when Maureen O'Mara was at the beck and call of a poodle. How're ye, Rosi?'

She held out her arms for a hug and Roisin stepped into the embrace, smelling her familiar biscuit and hairspray smell as she squeezed her back. 'I'm grand, Bronagh.' The older woman released her and studied her face.

'You look well. Your mammy told me you're doing ever so well with your new flat and job. Good for you.'

'Thanks.' It was nice to know Mammy had been singing her praises. 'I won't lie. It hasn't been easy but it's getting easier.'

Bronagh nodded. 'It's all very brave of you.'

Roisin the Brave. She liked how that sounded. It was a much better title than Easy-osi Rosi, she decided, wondering if she could get Mammy to run with it and then, remembering herself, she asked, 'And how are you, how's your mam doing?'

'Ah, she's much the same. We're looking forward to Christmas day though, it will be a lovely treat to have our dinner with you all.'

'It's lovely you're both coming.' Bronagh and her mammy were as good as family and Bronagh deserved to enjoy Christmas, to put her feet up for the day and have a good meal served up for her in the company of those that cared about her and her mammy. Roisin knew how hard she worked looking after her ailing mammy. In between that and working at O'Mara's there wasn't much time left over for anything else in Bronagh's life. Christmas dinner was to be had in the guesthouse dining room and Aisling had said they could decorate it and give it a festive feel on Christmas Eve before they went to Midnight Mass. There would be mulled wine, she'd added temptingly. Roisin wondered idly if Pooh was invited. Odds were, he would be. The way things were looking he'd probably be at the head of the table.

Bronagh checked her watch. 'Nina should be here any minute. I want to do a shop on the way home and if I time it right it shouldn't be too busy.'

'Is she going home to Spain for Christmas?'

'No, I don't think so. She said something a while back about the airfares being too expensive at this time of year. She's a lovely girl but she doesn't give much away.'

'I'd hate to think of her on her own at Christmas.' Roisin would ask Aisling if their Spanish night receptionist had been included on the Christmas invitation list and if not, she'd be sure to include her. It would be hard to be away from family at this time of year but airfares home would be at premium so she could understand why she was staying put.

Bronagh nodded her agreement sending the reindeer dancing once more and then lowered her voice to a conspiratorial level. Her tone implied they were all girls together as she asked, 'Any word from your fella?'

Roisin knew exactly to whom she was referring but she decided to play innocent. 'What fella, Bronagh? You've lost me.'

'You know,' her eyes glazed over, 'the tall, fine looking musician whose grumpy old granddad stayed with us. The one you had,' she made inverted finger signs, 'coffee with.'

'No, sorry, Bronagh, I'm not with you.'

Bronagh pressed her lips together; she didn't believe a word of it but looking past Roisin she spied Noah turning one of the gold boxes under the tree over in his hands. 'You'll not find much in them, young man. Sure, they're just there to look pretty. A bit like me, really.' She patted her jet-black shoulder-length hair and as she chortled away, thoroughly pleased with her little joke, Roisin noticed the telltale zebra stripe down her parting was gone. She'd had her hair done in time for Christmas. It made her pat her own, and wonder whether she should try and book in for a bit of a shampoo and blow-dry. She could do with a good cut, too. Her hair and its upkeep had been at the bottom of her list this last while and she knew it could do with some TLC. Mind you, it would be murder trying to get in anywhere this time of year but you never knew, someone might make a last-minute cancellation. She could always ring Jenny, her old pal from her very short-lived hairdressing days—she hadn't been a natural. Jenny owed her. It was her who'd offloaded Pooh on Mammy. Yes, she decided that's what she'd do.

Noah put the box down and mooched over toward his mammy with a disappointed expression. What was the point in having a box all done up in bows and ribbons and gold paper with nothing inside it?

'Ah now, no need for that face. You didn't think I'd let you come all the way from London without having a little something tucked away for you, now did you?'

The gold box was forgotten as he trotted over to where Bronagh had moved behind her desk. He craned his neck trying to see what it was she was getting out of her drawer. She held whatever it was behind her back. 'You know your old Aunty Bronagh expects a hug first so I do.'

Offer him a treat, and he was anybody's, Roisin thought, looking on as Noah wrapped his padded arms around her generous middle.

He let her go and looked up at her eagerly.

'Have you been a good boy for your mam?'

'I have.' Emphatic nodding followed.

'That's good to hear. Now then don't make yourself sick on it or your mammy will have words with me.'

'Thank you!' Noah squealed taking the Terry's Chocolate Orange. His favourite chocolate in the whole world.

'And remember don't tap it, whack it,' Bronagh quoted the old advert and winked over at Roisin. 'I should tell him not to give you so much as segment of it, keeping secrets from me.'

'I'm not.'

'Oh, I've been round the block a few times and I know that look you got on your face when I mentioned his name. It's the same expression you had when you started seeing that fella with the motorbike your parents couldn't stand and you'd sneak out to meet him. I'll find out what the story is. I've got my sources you know. Your Moira's very partial to a Terry's Chocolate Orange, if my memory serves me rightly.'

'Bribery, Bronagh, that's terrible so it is!'

'Needs must,' she muttered as Noah began to tell her all about Mr Nibbles and his anxiety-driven bowel issues when it came to air travel.

'Serves you right,' Roisin whispered, leaving them to it and calling back over her shoulder, 'Send him up when he's finished, Bronagh!' She took the stairs two at a time. It was quiet in the guesthouse at this time of the day with most of the guests still out and about exploring. The landings were deserted, and Ita, the young girl in charge of housekeeping—Idle Ita as Moira called her—would be long gone for the day. This in-between time of day had always been Roisin's favourite when she was a child, she and her siblings had had the best games of hide-and-seek when they'd had the run of the old place.

The stairs creaked as she headed up the last flight to the family's apartment. Home, she thought, pushing the door open and hearing her youngest sister shrieking, 'Get that fecking dog away from me, Mammy, I mean it!' Yes, she was home.

Chapter 9

Roisin walked into a scene whereby Pooh had Moira trapped up against the kitchen worktop and Aisling was bent double laughing as she said, 'Your face, I wish I had a camera.' Maureen was already ensconced on the sofa like the Queen Mother and was patting her leg trying to get Pooh to come hither. 'Mammy, if you don't get off your arse and get him off me right now, I'm not going to let you have any dessert.'

'What is it?'

'A New York cheesecake, Marks and Spencer's.'

'Ah now, Moira, that's not fair. You know the New York one is my favourite.'

'Well, sort your dog! Stop licking me you, you... and you can stop laughing.' That was aimed at Aisling.

'Rosi! How're you?' Aisling got to her sister first for a hello hug. They were elbowed aside by Maureen as she took action, taking Pooh by his collar and steering him into the living room towards a bed identical to the one at her apartment.

Roisin and Moira embraced and then Roisin stood back looking from sister to sister. 'You're both looking really well.'

'It's because we're getting some.'

'I heard that!' Maureen said sitting back down.

Roisin laughed. 'Well all the riding obviously agrees with you both.' The banter made her think of Shay but she vanquished him by staring at the red onion Moira had been slicing into for the salad before the Pooh assault. She didn't want to be caught out by her eagle-eyed sisters, one grilling from Mammy had been quite enough!

Maureen made them all jump by shrieking, 'Jaysus, Mary and Joseph, four hundred and fifty pound for the privilege of swanning about in your nightie.' She was holding up one of Aisling's glossy fashion mags and on inspection the model pouting at the camera did look like she was in her nightie, Roisin decided. A nice one, but still a nightie.

Moira muttered, 'I don't think you are in a position to comment on the world of fashion because the last time I checked, pants that could stop the blood supply to your bits were not in vogue. Where did you get them from and who told you they looked good?'

Roisin and Aisling sniggered waiting for Moira to get told off but Mammy hadn't heard—she was too busy flicking the pages of the magazine.

'They are on the snug side,' Aisling said, and Moira snorted.

'Snug? Sure, I can see what she had for breakfast. One wrong move and she'll have the arse out of them. How could you let her out of the house, Rosi? It's disgraceful so it is.'

'When did anyone ever talk Mammy out of anything?'

'True.' Her sisters nodded, each lost in their own recollections of run-ins with their headstrong mammy.

Roisin explained to them both how their mammy had come to be wearing yoga pants a couple of sizes too small for her, getting a sympathetic tut from them both at the way she'd hustled them off her. 'She pinched my new teal River Island sweater the other week. It'll be all baggy around the boobs by the time I get it back,' Moira moaned.

'Well, all I can say is watch your knickers girls, she's on about giving the thong a whirl.'

'Ewww!' The pair of them grimaced.

'What are you lot on about in there?'

'Nothing, Mammy.'

Noah burst through the door at that moment, bouncing in to give his aunties a cuddle before taking a great big gulp of air to begin another round of the gerbil chronicles.

Roisin helped herself to two glasses of the red Aisling was obviously enjoying, given the purple stain on her lips. She saw the glass of Coke fizzing on the bench by the salad the pair of them were in the throes of tossing together. Moira was still on the wagon then, she thought approvingly, hoping Noah didn't spot it. He'd be like one of those old Alvin and the Chipmunks records if he got stuck into the fizz. She carried the wine over to the sofa and handing Mammy the long-stemmed glass she plonked down next to her. 'Something smells good, doesn't it?' She took a sip, savouring the aroma as Moira opened the oven to check on the contents, sending a thick garlicky aroma wafting over.

'Moira's on dinner and she'll tell you she's after making it from scratch but don't believe a word of it. I saw the box in the bin. It's a Marks and Spencer's family sized lasagne. I hope it's not too heavy on the garlic,' Maureen sniffed. 'Garlic gives me reflux.' She patted her chest.

Roisin smiled, not about the reflux because a windy Mammy was nothing to smile about, but at Moira's lack of prowess in the kitchen despite Mammy's best efforts to teach her how to cook over the years. Ah well, so long as she got fed, she didn't care what was put in front of her. The walk along the pier had left her ravenous. She enjoyed a few more sips of wine and then, as Noah moseyed over with a piece of garlic bread in his hand, she got up to see if she could snaffle a piece.

'Oh no, you don't.' Aisling slapped her hand. 'I only gave it to Noah to stop him going on about that Mr Nibbles of his. He told me we'll get the privilege of actually meeting him when you come and stay on Christmas Eve. I can't wait.'

'It was Colin's big idea to get him a gerbil.'

'Always said he was a chinless feck,' Moira piped up.

'Shush. Big ears are always flapping,'

'Whose Noah's or Mammy's?' Aisling asked.

'Both.' Roisin leaned against the kitchen counter. 'Guess what happened when we went for a walk down the pier with Pooh this afternoon.'

As Moira began dishing out the lasagne and Aisling broke up the garlic bread, Roisin made them both laugh with her impersonation of a Scandinavian woman using bad language.

'That poodle has behavioural issues,' Moira said, then, indicating the cutlery drawer, 'You could set the table, Rosi.'

Roisin did so while Noah petted Pooh who was lying with his head resting on his paws. His doggy face in repose looked like butter wouldn't melt. 'Go and wash your hands, Noah, we'll be eating in a minute.'

Her son huffed and puffed out of the room narrowly missing his Aunty Moira who was carrying two heaped plates of food over to the table. Pooh waited until they were all seated and Maureen had said the grace before getting up and wandering over to the table. He sat at Aisling's feet having decided she was likely the softest touch and stared up at her with huge baleful eyes begging for a morsel. 'Mammy, he's making me feel ever so guilty.'

'Ignore him, Aisling, he could win an Oscar for his role in Starving Dog, so he could.' Maureen tutted, forking up the mince and pasta dish enthusiastically.

'This is delicious, Moira,' Roisin said, winking across the table at her mammy and receiving a 'Don't talk with your mouth full, Rosi,' in return.

Noah's eyes whizzed from one family member to the other, unused to so much banter at the dinner table.

Roisin caught up on her sisters' news as she tucked into her meal. Moira was immersed in her course at the National College of Art and Design and after an initial rocky start as she got used to being a student and no longer having a disposable income, she was loving it. She and Tom were getting along very well and before she could launch into exactly how well, Mammy interrupted by asking her to pass the salt. Aisling was kept busy ensuring the smooth turning of the cogs at O'Mara's during the day and was spending most of her evenings at Quinn's these days. 'Shay was asking after you last week when his band was playing. I told him you were coming home for Christmas. Meaningful and inuendo-laden glances were exchanged around the table but with Noah at the table nobody said a word on the subject. Roisin adopted her best, 'So what?' expression as her stomach did flip-flops. *He'd been asking after her. He knew she was going to be home. Perhaps she could leave it all to fate and just see what happened.* She realised Aisling was speaking. 'What did you think of the Californian Giant Redwood on display downstairs?'

'It's gorgeous but it is big, you'll have problems fitting everyone in reception if you have any large groups due to arrive.'

'It's a health and safety hazard, is what it is,' Aisling muttered, before adding she hadn't a show of getting anything smaller. There was no getting around Bronagh once she'd her heart set on something and her heart had been very firmly set on the biggest tree she could find. 'She talked one of the tour operators into putting it in their van and delivering it for her, bribed them with a custard cream and a cup of tea, so she did.'

'Now then girls.' Maureen changed the subject. 'I'd like us to visit with Father Christmas tomorrow.'

Moira sniggered and Roisin and Aisling glanced at each other, silently communicating the words, 'What the feck is she on about now?'

'I'd like to get a family photograph taken with Noah on yer man's knee and us girls can gather around them. I happen to know Father Christmas is in his grotto at the O'Connell Street, Easons.' She closed her eyes. 'I can picture it. It will be lovely to have as a keepsake.'

'I can picture it too, and I'm seeing short red dresses and Santa hats and it's not happening, Mammy.'

'Don't lower the tone, Moira, sure it's Father Christmas we're talking about here not yer man who runs all those seedy London nightclubs.'

'Peter Stringfellow,' Aisling added helpfully.

'That's him, dirty old man, so he is.'

'I want to go and see Father Christmas,' Noah chimed in.

'There we go then, that's settled. Tomorrow afternoon. Let's say two o'clock, and I don't want any excuses. You'll not spoil things for Noah here.'

Nana and grandson looked smugly complicit. He reached over the table for the last piece of garlic bread while his aunties engaged in moaning about being grown women and having to sit on Santa's knee. His nana was lobbing back that the only one sitting on his knee, thank you very much, would be Noah, when a commotion began.

Pooh woofed, startling them all silent, before getting up and stalking toward the front door, a low growl emanating from his throat. The O'Mara women looked to one another. It was peculiar behaviour. He began to bark in earnest and they all jumped as they heard the front door bang shut.

'Who's there?' Maureen called, 'State your business.'

If the sisters hadn't been feeling nervous, they would have giggled at their mammy's turn of phrase. Pooh had begun to go berserk and all the guests would be complaining about the noise, and so Maureen bravely stood up to investigate but before she could remove herself from the table a voice boomed.

'Whoever's dog this is would you tell it to get its nose the hell out of my girlfriend's crotch?'

Eyes widened and Maureen disappeared like a lightning streak in the direction of the voice.

'So,' Aisling said, looking at Roisin and Moira, 'the prodigal son's returned home for Christmas.'

Chapter 10

He looked good, in a slick American sort of way, Roisin thought, as her brother, larger than life, appeared in the living room. Mammy was hanging off his arm and gazing up at him as though the Messiah himself had wandered into the apartment. Mercifully for Patrick he'd escaped the short gene of the O'Mara women taking after their daddy. Mammy, Roisin saw, had a firm hold of Pooh's collar with her other hand. He'd always been a good-looking fella their brother and well aware of the fact too. He'd been good fun as well when they were kids. Now though it was as if his features had gotten a little more chiselled, his hair a little more groomed during his time in the States. Everything about him seemed exaggerated. As for his teeth, well they'd definitely gotten whiter. If you were to sit in a darkened cinema with him all you'd see were the whites of his eyes and those pearlies. It would be like when that awful ultra-violet light would flicker at nightclubs and show the flecks of dandruff on your shoulders. She suspected her brother's new improved smile wasn't down to flossing and twice daily use of the Colgate either.

She continued her inspection. His skin had a healthy sun-kissed glow about it, making the rest of his family look like relations of Casper the friendly Ghost, and his clothes had the casually, crumpled cool of the confident man. The man who didn't have to prove anything to anyone, he was his own boss. *For fecks sake, Rosi, you're not doing an aftershave commercial.*

She knew though, if he wasn't her brother and if he wasn't such a selfish arse at times, she would say he cut a fine figure of a man. All her and Aisling's friends had thought so back in the day. It had been very annoying.

A woman materialised from behind Mammy and son. She was wearing a fitted, short pink dress not fit for the Irish winter. It hugged every inch of her upper torso and could rival the snugness of Mammy's yoga pants. Roisin's eyes were mesmerised by the twin peaks jutting forth, like two watermelons, disproportionate to the woman's slender figure. Aisling and Moira were staring too, jaws agape. The woman was keeping a wary distance from the excitable poodle who kept twisting his head trying to catch another glimpse of his paramour. Roisin managed to raise her eyes to stare at the tanned, golden blonde apparition's face. No wonder Pooh had gone to town, he'd found his dream girl. Patrick's girlfriend, Cindy, was in fact, Barbie. Come to think of it her brother did have a look of that Ken doll he'd been so fond of talking to when he was small. They were a good match.

'Look who's here, girls,' Maureen stated the obvious, 'your brother. He's home for Christmas. Sure, it's the best present any mammy could have and he's brought his girlfriend, Cindy, with him.'

Patrick looked down at his mammy and Mammy gazed up at her son and Roisin knew Aisling was choking back gagging noises. Mammy had a short-term memory when it came to her son. They'd barely heard a word since he'd flounced off back to Los Angeles, a sulky, spoiled child after not getting his way over O'Mara's being sold. Roisin had always sat on the fence where her brother was concerned. Yes, he looked out for number one but she only had one brother and she loved him. He'd pushed her over into Aisling's school of thought though, with his behaviour this last year. Had he contacted any of them to see how they were getting on? No, he had not, and there was poor Moira who'd been on the sauce making a mess of things. Aisling, too had been heartbroken when that eejit fiancé of hers left her high and dry. Not to mention herself with a marriage break-up and Mammy laid up for weeks with a broken ankle. Now here he was standing there with that irritating smug look she knew so well, waiting to be made a fuss of. Well, he could feck off, she thought.

Moira, who'd always thought the sun rose and set over her brother, forgot she was annoyed at feeling like he'd abandoned her and she was the first up, throwing her arms around him. The Coca-Cola had gone to her head, Roisin thought, suddenly remembering her manners where his poor girlfriend was concerned. 'Hello there, Cindy. Welcome to O'Mara's. I'm Roisin and this is my son, Noah.' She got up from the table and stepped forward to kiss her brother's girlfriend on the cheek, receiving a grateful, boob squishy, embrace in return. She smelled like fruity chewing gum, and vanilla and if she hadn't been full it would have made her hungry. Aisling followed suit while Moira joined in with Patrick and Mammy's mutual admiration society. Poor Cindy would have a hard time getting a look-in with these two on the scene, Roisin thought, giving Noah a nudge to say hello. She looked down at him, seeing he was starstruck with a very silly look on his face not dissimilar to Pooh's, as he whispered a shy greeting.

'Hey there, honey, aren't you just the cutest wee man.'

Roisin watched on amused as her son flushed at the praise.

'It was Patrick's idea to surprise you.' She addressed the sisters. Her drawl was more southern than LA and Roisin instantly thought of fried chicken and had to squash the urge to say, Y'all c'mon back now, y'hear.

'Well, you did that. Here, come and sit down, make yourself at home. No, don't worry about him. I'll make sure Mammy keeps an eye on him.' Roisin gave a Pooh the death stare as she led Cindy over to the sofa. Aisling offered her a drink but she didn't want anything. She looked the type that would keep a watchful eye on her waistline, Roisin decided, a sparkling water and egg white omelette sort of a girl. She couldn't afford not to be if the dress she was poured into was an indicator as to the rest of her wardrobe. Ha! Just wait until Mrs Flaherty got hold of her! O'Mara's breakfast cook, believed diet to be a dirty word and you did not mess with Mrs Flaherty.

Patrick extricated himself from his mammy and Moira long enough to give his other two sisters a hello kiss and hug. 'Aisling, you're looking very well on it.'

Aisling eyed him suspiciously. She was never sure whether you're looking very well on it meant she looked like she'd been eating all the pies or not.

'And I was sorry to hear about you and Colin, Rosi. I hope you're doing okay?'

'Ah, sure.' Roisin waved the comment away. 'We're grand.'

Patrick turned to Noah who was looking at him uncertainly. 'Now then, young fella, have you a hug for your Uncle Patrick who's flown all the way from America?'

'I've got a gerbil,' Noah said, testing the water. 'His name's Mr Nibbles.'

'That's a fine sounding name for a gerbil,' Patrick said, receiving a hug. He was easily bought her son, Roisin thought, not for the first time as her brother pulled a tube of M&M's from his pocket and gave them to Noah.

'Come on and sit down,' Maureen urged, patting the space between her and Moira they had left for him to squeeze into. He did so.

'Rosi, Aisling, go and see that your brother's room's made up and put his and Cindy's bags in there while you're at it. We're all very modern here,' she added.

Roisin resisted the urge to tell Mammy nobody had chopped Patrick's legs off. She supposed he had just flown in from LA though. Just this once, she thought, and she begrudgingly followed her equally begrudging sister from the room. Noah seized the opportunity to sit next to Cindy, delighted to secure a position next to her and certain she would be the type of girl who would love gerbils and not the type to try and pinch the M&M's off him.

'WHY DO YOU THINK HE'S back?' Roisin said, tucking in her corner of the bed and smoothing the sheet.

Aisling did the same. 'I don't know but if he's any plans of putting the squeeze on Mammy about selling O'Mara's again, I'll personally stick him in a box and send him back to Los Angeles with a do not return sticker.'

'Ah, Ash, maybe we should give him the benefit of the doubt. You know maybe he just misses us and thought it would be nice to spend Christmas with his family. Or, maybe things are getting serious between him and Cindy and he thought he should introduce her to us all.'

Aisling sighed. 'Rosi, it's Patrick you're talking about. The only person Patrick's ever had a deep and meaningful relationship with is himself. No, he'll have one of his deals on the go, it'll be business that's brought him back, not us.'

'You're too cynical,' Roisin said, although her sister's description of their brother was bang on. 'What did you make of Cindy?' she asked, pausing in her stuffing of the pillow into the case. 'I think she seems sweet, but I can't stop staring at her breasts.'

'Me neither, they're enormous, but sure, she must be used to it. There's no way they're natural. I reckon she went along to yer plastic surgeon one and said, 'I'll have the Pam Anderson special please, and speaking of unnatural. Who am I?' Aisling cracked a cheesy grin and said, 'Ah, Mammy, you're the best mammy in the whole world and I'm a fecky big brown noser, so I am.'

Roisin giggled. 'Pat. The state of those teeth. Honest to God any whiter you'd want to wear sunglasses around him.'

Aisling plumped her pillow and put it on the bed. 'It will be strange having him back in his old room.

'I wonder if you'll hear the old headboard banging.' Roisin pointed to it.

'That's disgusting, so it is. Besides I'm off round to Quinn's later and Moira's going to Tom's so Pat and Ms Pneumatic Breasts can bang away to their hearts delight, but I won't be changing the sheets at the end of the week.' She paused in her smoothing of the eiderdown. 'How does Mammy seem to you?'

'Oh, you know, Mammy's Mammy.'

'You don't think she seems a little,' Aisling cast about for the word she was looking for. 'Preoccupied?'

'I hadn't noticed. Why?'

'I don't know. She had dinner at the yacht club a weekend or so back. She got her hair done and everything for it because it was quite a posh do she reckons, and she's been wandering around with her head in the clouds since. Moira reckons she's after meeting a fella.'

'No!' The thought of Mammy with anyone other than their daddy was a bizarre one, but it was over two years since he'd passed now and while their mammy was their mammy, she was also a woman in her own right. That was a bizarre thought too! 'Although she did say there was dancing and that she'd had a grand time.'

'Well, something's up and she's not saying whatever it is but when I quizzed as to how her night was, she was very cagey. She had that look on her face, you know, the one where she's after borrowing something like your lipstick, or—'

'Yoga pants and I know the look well.'

'Yeah,' Aisling smiled.

'How would you feel about it if she did meet someone?' Roisin probed.

'Weird at first, I guess, but she has every right to be happy and it wouldn't mean she loved Daddy any less.'

'No, you're right. I hadn't thought about it like that but it wouldn't.'

'Moira surprised me because you know how much of a daddy's girl she was. I always thought she'd struggle if Mammy did meet anyone else but she was kind of nonchalant about it all. That trip to Vietnam changed her. For the better too.'

'Who'd have thought?'

'I know, and I suppose I'm getting ahead of myself. We don't know she *has* met anyone but with all the clubs she belongs to she's bound to hook up with a merry widower at some point.'

'Yes, I suppose she is.'

They finished their task in silence and then Roisin remembered the dessert. 'Do you reckon, Moira's cut into the cheesecake yet?' Seeing as she was the only sibling who would not be doing any riding tonight, she planned to compensate with a big helping.

'I hope not, I want to make sure she doesn't give Patrick a bigger slice than me.'

On that note they took themselves off back to the living room.

WHAT A STRANGE TURN the evening had taken, Roisin thought, wiping the last of the dishes dry as Aisling, the washing up done, began making everybody coffee. Patrick was regaling them with stories about life in the LA fast lane while Mammy sat on one side of him on the sofa, Moira on the other, hanging off his every word. Poor Cindy was squished down the end next to Mammy and hadn't taken her eyes off Pooh; her legs were tightly crossed. Neither Pooh nor Noah who was sprawled on the carpet, elbows resting on the floor, chin cupped in his hands, had taken their eyes off Cindy.

It was then that her phone began to vibrate in her pocket and pulling it out she expected it to be Colin wanting to know they'd arrived safe and sound. It wasn't Colin though. It was Shay.

Chapter 11
Clio

Clio stared down at the card, open on the table in front of her, almost afraid to read the words squeezed around the bog-standard Christmas greeting. The phone ringing in the hallway jolted her from her trance. 'You're being silly, Clio, old girl. It was over four decades ago. And you can sod off.' She directed the latter at the telephone. It was probably Mags, her agent, and she could wait. Sure, if it was that important, she'd call back she decided, waiting for it to ring off. She'd always thought the literary agent's role was to support their author but Clio felt as though she were the one keeping Mags on an even keel since the book had hit the shelves. When her house was once more bathed in silence apart from him next door's motorcycle engine revving off into the distance she began to read.

Dear Clio,

I realise this card will be a bolt from the blue but when I read the review of your book in the Irish Times I had to write and congratulate you. You always said you'd write a novel that would be a bestseller and now you've only gone and done it! Congratulations, what an achievement. Of course, I rushed straight out and bought a copy which I devoured over three days. It's wonderful, but Harry and Lyssa's story raised a lot of questions because I can't help but wonder if you wrote it about us. Or am I being arrogant? That's something I've been accused of before. I still live in

Boston in case you were wondering but I've always liked to keep my finger on the pulse of what was happening in Dublin. I've subscribed to the Times for over forty years. I followed your reporting and well-written pieces with interest over the years too. I miss stumbling across them. I always felt inordinately proud when I'd see your name in the byline. I'd want to nudge the person on the train next to me and tell them that I knew you when you were a girl. And that you were the most feisty, determined woman I ever met. I'm going to run out of room and there's so much more I'd like to say. The thing is, Clio, I'm writing to you because I'm coming back. Your story made me nostalgic for all my old haunts from that wonderful year and now that I have finally hung my hat up and retired, the time is ripe. I arrive on the afternoon of the 24th and I would like to invite you to share Christmas dinner with me. I have made a booking for two at the Merrion Hotel in the Garden Room at one o'clock and will be waiting in the Drawing Room at 12.45pm. Please don't think me presumptuous, merely hopeful.

Yours, hopefully,

Gerry.

Clio's tea had gone cold and her toast, although filling the air with its malty aroma, was long since popped and had been forgotten about. The almost milky scent of fresh toast usually filled her with a sense that all was well in her world just as cigarettes once had. Oh, how she used to eat the things when she was working! She'd given up before it had a chance to catch up with her though. Right now though, feeling as though her world had been upended, she'd kill for one. Gerry had always had that effect on her but she'd been too young to know better then. At eighteen her defences had been down and she'd had a trusting openness to seize all the possibilities life had to offer her. Now she was a fifty-nine-year-old woman who should know better than to allow her breath to quicken and pulse to race at the memory of the man she'd once loved with her whole being. A man whose heart she'd had to break.

A thought struck her then, rather like the stinging slap her mother wielded to the back of her legs when she'd been cheeky as a child. 'He won't look like you remember him, Clio. He's been forever frozen in your mind as he was but time hasn't stood still. He's a pensioner, old girl.' It was swiftly followed by the realisation that she no longer had the dewy skin of a girl on the cusp of womanhood. She too was rapidly approaching her pensionable years, unless of course the government pushed back the age for hanging one's hat up as they'd been making noises of doing. Of course, it made no bones to her. She was a long way from putting her hat anywhere other than firmly on her head. Still, fifty-nine, how on earth did that happen?

How did one go from being a girl who thought she had the right to have it all to being a woman who now thought nothing of holding a discussion with herself?

She remembered how bereft she'd been when Gerry left. He'd never lied to her. He'd never made promises he couldn't keep, but she'd been swept along by the heady tide of first love and had believed that somehow it would all work out. It hadn't and it had been her fault. She'd decided to throw herself into her work at the paper, dragging herself up the rungs of the ladder in a male dominated era. It hadn't been easy. It had taken her fifteen years to smash through that glass ceiling. She'd known when she'd had to make her choice that it was sink or swim time for her career and she'd chosen to swim. Gerry Byrne and his family obligations would not sink her.

It *was* presumptuous on his part to assume she would drop everything and have her Christmas dinner with him. How did he know she didn't have a family who were desperate for her to be a part of their festivities? Sure, there was Fidelma and her lot expecting her. She'd spent every Christmas with her sister's brood since Mam passed. Fidelma's children, although now adults with children of their own, would surely miss their aunt if she weren't there? She'd spoiled them enough over the years to warrant the title of 'favourite aunty'.

Clio's neatly trimmed nails, a must when one spent the majority of one's time on a typewriter, drummed the table. She wouldn't think about it anymore. She would tuck the card away in the top drawer of her sideboard over there and she would bin the cold toast and make some more. She'd have her breakfast and begin her day. 'You've a novel you're supposed to be writing, Clio. You've a deadline to make and you do not have time for Gerry Byrne to come-a-calling. You're going to pretend you never received his card. It went missing in the post, so it did, like hundreds of letters and cards do at this time of the year. There, problem solved.' As she pushed her seat back and stood up, she didn't believe a word she'd just said.

Chapter 12

'I better not see anybody I know,' Moira grumbled, flicking her hair back over her shoulder as they elbowed their way into Easons. 'I feel like a complete eejit next to you lot.'

'Odds are you will then. That's what always happens. It's like when you nip out to Tesco's with no make-up on and your rattiest Sunday sloth clothes and there's your arch nemesis from the high school looking like they're off clubbing.' Aisling was embittered by personal experience. She pointed through the sea of faces. 'Oh look, speaking of high school, isn't that your old school pal, Emma, over there? You know the one who fancied herself as Ginger Spice getting around in that Union Jack T-shirt.'

'Where?!' Moira looked panicked as she stared around at the sea of faces.

'I'm joking with you.'

'Oh, feck off, Ash.'

'You feel like an eejit, Moira, because you look like one. We all do,' Roisin stated, keeping a tight hold of Noah's hand. It was a mosh pit of mammies and their offspring in here. She glanced down at her son; even he looked eejitty in his crew neck, red sweater. He reminded her a little of Charlie, from their favourite Christmas film Charlie and the Chocolate Factory. His nana had presented the sweater to him this morning and combed his hair into a smooth side parting rather than leave it to stand on end like Roisin did. She'd had one of her golfing ladies, a prolific knitter, whip the cable patterned red, sweater up specially for him.

'It itches, Mummy, do I have to wear it?' he'd whispered in her ear.

'What do you think?' she replied, gesturing at his nana who was singing her heart out to Mariah Carey's *All I Want for Christmas* on the radio as she waited for her toast to pop. He'd slunk off miserably to play with Mr Nibbles. Poor love looked like it was choking him, she thought now. Mammy had insisted, in a way that brooked no argument, on them all wearing red tops and blue jeans for this, their family Christmas photo.

Red, she'd declared last night over coffee and the after dinner mints Patrick had picked up in duty free, was festive and the blue jeans added the perfect casual accompaniment. She didn't want the photograph to look contrived. All three sisters had said, 'Bollocks,' in reply to this and Roisin could tell Cindy would have liked to have joined in with the sentiment but was too intimidated by Mammy to do so. Patrick had said a family photo sounded just the ticket and Roisin had heard Aisling mumble her favourite phrase where her brother was concerned, 'brown nosey fecker,' under her breath as she helped herself to two of the chocolate mints before stuffing them both in her mouth. Aisling always ate when she was feeling stressed.

'We look like we're a family band, you know like the Corrs except we're not cool,' Aisling said, now nibbling on the chocolate chip muesli bar she'd stashed in her handbag for emergency situations. Being forced out in public wearing matching outfits with her mammy, nephew, siblings and her brother's girlfriend counted as such.

'Or like we've stepped out of the television screen from some cheesy family sitcom,' Roisin said. 'We're the Keatons from *Family Ties*, remember that show?'

'Bags be Mallory,' Aisling said through her mouthful.

Roisin ignored her. 'Mammy always used to say, why couldn't we be more like the Keaton family and sort our problems out without all the bickering, remember?' She rolled her eyes at the memory.

'I do. It was very annoying.' Aisling sniggered as she pointed at Patrick's back ahead of her. 'And there's ole Michael J. Fox over there.' He'd had to shoot off down to Grafton Street earlier that morning with Cindy to get something suitably red for them both to wear—there was no chance of Cindy getting that chest of hers inside anything the O'Mara women owned. Although suitable was a term that could be used loosely when it came to Cindy's choice of plunging red mesh top and jeans that had Mammy whispering in the sisters' ears, would need to be surgically removed at the after hours later on.

Aisling glanced down at her filmy blouse; it was chiffon, the sort of thing she wouldn't normally be seen dead in. It reeked of Arpège, Mammy's signature fragrance. She'd thrust it at her earlier that morning when she'd arrived at O'Mara's with Roisin and Noah meekly following behind announcing she'd come early to ensure her wardrobe instructions were obeyed. 'It's alright for you three, red suits you with your colouring but it makes me look like I've picked up some sort of chronic disease.' She'd not been happy, telling Moira to shut up when she smirked at the state of her in the blouse. Mammy had told her she'd better be careful or the wind would change and she'd be stuck with a face on her like a gin-soaked prune forever. Roisin had got off lightly, borrowing a turtle neck from Moira that looked very well on her and Moira looked the part in her preppy red jacket.

'We're the fecking Addams family,' Moira added her pennies' worth. 'And there's Morticia,' she pointed at Mammy, who had—thank the Lord—opted for chinos with her red shirt.

'The Bundys, and Mammy's Peg Bundy.' Aisling giggled getting into it now, and Moira and Roisin joined in.

'No, I've got it.' Roisin jiggled on the spot. 'The Waltons.' This time there was proper giggling as Aisling and Roisin chimed, 'John Boy' as they pointed at their brother. Roisin began humming the theme tune.

Mammy looked back over her shoulder. 'What are you three on about.'

'Nothing, Mammy.' Moira smiled sweetly. 'Just saying what a grand idea of yours this was.'

Maureen narrowed her eyes, unsure if she was picking up on sarcasm in her youngest daughter's tone or not.

'I suppose we should be grateful she didn't try and bring Pooh along in a little red doggy coat for the occasion,' Roisin said, once Mammy had returned to her chat with Patrick. She'd had to have words with Noah who'd been desperate to introduce Father Christmas to Mr Nibbles. She'd only managed to dissuade him by saying that if Mr Nibbles got frightened and had an accident, Father Christmas might not be too happy about it and it could possibly have a roll-on effect as to what appeared in Noah's Christmas stocking.

'Oi, you.' Moira nudged Roisin as she recalled her sister's flushed face and coy expression upon answering her phone last night. 'Who was that you were speaking to last night. I know it wasn't Colin because you always get this screwed up expression on your face like you've got the piles when you talk to him, and I know it wasn't a friend because your voice went all sort of low and Macy Gray like. My money's on Mr Hot Fiddle.'

Roisin hesitated, she didn't want to share her phone call with her sisters. She wanted to keep her exchange with Shay tucked away to bring out in private to mull over. Not that privacy was a big feature on her trips home! Every time she recalled the melodic timbre of his voice, heat shunted through her core and the feeling that evoked was not one she wanted her family privy to for obvious reasons. It had taken her by surprise, him calling so soon after she'd arrived back in Dublin, his obvious interest only adding to the thrill of listening to him ask how life in London was treating her. She'd seen her sisters' curious glances as she told him she'd found work, and a new flat for her and Noah. She'd glared over at them before turning her back on her all-seeing, all-hearing family.

They hadn't talked for long, he was due to go on stage in a few minutes having left the rest of the band warming up and it was the first chance he'd had all day to give her a call. The way he'd said 'stage' conjured an image of his rangy body clothed in a blue plaid shirt, the sleeves of which were rolled up, the buttons undone to reveal a smooth muscular chest, and his faded Levi's battered and worn with a brown leather belt. The cowboy hat was dipped low over one eye and his thumbs were hooked through his belt loops. She realised she'd seen a book cover not dissimilar to the scenario she was envisaging at Mammy's and quickly banished it. He played Irish folk music and rock not country and western and he was not the type of man to walk around Dublin with a cowboy hat on.

Standing there in the kitchen she'd suddenly wanted to see him performing more than anything. To sit down the back of the crowded pub he was gigging at and just watch him. A door had banged then and she'd heard music and shouts of laughter in the background. He'd said he had to go but before he hung up he asked her if she'd like to catch up for a drink or dinner before Christmas, whatever she could squeeze in because he knew it was short notice and she'd be busy given the time of the year. She could manage dinner tomorrow evening she said, hoping she hadn't sounded too eager.

She was already imagining the feel of his knee as she accidentally on purpose grazed hers against his under the table. They'd said their goodbyes with him arranging to pick her up from O'Mara's at seven. She was certain Mammy or one of her siblings would have Noah although she didn't relish telling them where she was going. She'd held the phone to her ear for a few more seconds after the call had disconnected, putting the parts of herself that had disassembled at the sound of his voice back together before joining the others in the living room once more.

Now, standing in the heaving book shop, Moira nudged her again. 'Well, was it, Shay?'

'Ow, don't do that.'

Aisling moved closer to hear what Roisin had to say.

'Who's Shay, Mummy?'

She shot Moira a look. 'He's an old friend of Mummy's.'

Noah was nonplussed but Moira took the hint for the time being and dropped the subject.

TWENTY MINUTES LATER, tensions outside Santa's grotto were running high and even Patrick was beginning to make noises of dissent. 'Could we not just gather outside on the street and ask someone to take a photograph, Mammy?' he asked.

Maureen was aghast. 'With no Father Christmas?'

'We could get one of those random Santas that stand on the street corners.'

The withering look Patrick received saw him back down. He winced and rubbed his temples as a toddler somewhere in the midden began to screech, 'No, Santa. No like! NOOOOO!' A baby, fed up with the waiting and startled by the sudden outburst, began to shriek and the mammies, all determined to get a photograph of their precious offspring with Father Christmas, were beginning to look in need of gin.

The line they'd found themselves in shuffled forward every now and then and Roisin watched enviously as a victorious mammy herded her four immaculately dressed children past. Each was sucking a lollypop and clutching a balloon. She didn't have to turn around to know the victorious expression would have been wiped clean from her face when a loud pop made them all jump. It was followed by a howl that suggested the ended of the world was nigh. 'My balloon! I want another one. Mammy, I want another one. It's not fair! Eva, Connor and Mary have all got theirs.'

Oh yes, she thought, Christmas was a precious time for families.

Mammy swung around and jabbed at Moira, 'I remember you putting on a holy show like that when your balloon popped the year I took you to meet Father Christmas at Brown Thomas. Mortifying it was.'

Moira was unrepentant. 'Well, I'd say you're getting payback now, Mammy, wouldn't you?'

'Mummy,' Noah tugged on Roisin's sleeve. 'I can smell poo.'

Ah Jaysus, Roisin thought, her son was to the number two what David Attenborough was to the animal kingdom. He was getting obsessed and it was all down to Colin trying to get one up on her with the gerbil. She sniffed the air cautiously and at first all she could smell was too many women wearing too many clashing perfumes which mingled cloyingly together. Hang on, she thought, sniffing again and this time hit with the unmistakable smell of filled nappy. *Oh, dear God, could this afternoon get any worse!*

'Can you smell that,' Moira nudged her. 'Sure, it's worse than Mammy when she's been at the Brussels.' She deliberately said this loud enough to turn heads.

'I heard that,' Maureen said. 'Don't believe a word of it, Cindy. She's a one for making things up.'

This was a living nightmare, Roisin thought, shaking her head and wondering when she'd wake up.

At last, after forty-five or so minutes of unspeakable noise and smells, Santa's helper, who was keeping guard at the entrance to the grotto, came into their line of sight. She was a fierce looking girl with a frizz of red hair who looked as happy with her short red dress with white fur trim and matching hat as Aisling did with her blouse. Her arms were crossed over her chest, and stout, black-booted legs assumed the stance of a nightclub bouncer as she stood squarely in the entrance to the glittering cave where the end to their torment lay. Mechanical reindeer were positioned on either side of the grotto, heads bobbing slowly to the incessant Christmas carols being piped through the building.

'Would you look at the face on her,' Mammy hissed over her shoulder. 'Sure, she'd put the fear of God into you so she would.'

'Shush, Mammy, she'll hear you and send us to the back of the queue,' Aisling hissed back.

Roisin looked at her brother and Cindy, who were almost catatonic with the jet leg and the ordeal they were suffering through. Poor, poor Cindy, she'd put money on Patrick not having warned her what she was in for by coming to visit his family.

And then at last, like the parting of the red sea, the fierce one stepped aside and gestured for them to enter Father Christmas's inner sanctum.

Chapter 13

'Ho-ho-ho and who've we got here,' boomed Father Christmas from his gilt throne. A feeling of calm descended over the O'Mara group as they ducked through the glittery entrance and emerged into a peaceful Christmas bubble. The air felt fresh, thanks to the little fan blowing gently in the corner of the grotto. Faux presents were stacked up on either side of the big man's chair and a Christmas tree laden with red baubles dominated the small space. Roisin peered closely at him wanting to see if he was a nice, plump, jolly Santa or one of those skinny ones who looked nothing like your man. This one obviously liked his food, she thought, spying the crumbs stuck in his beard. It bode well; they were off to a good start after the nightmare of the shop floor outside. A young woman stepped out from behind a camera tripod. She was dressed identically to the fearsome helper on the door but looked much nicer insomuch that she at least mustered a weary smile even if it didn't quite reach her eyes.

Mammy was the family's self-appointed spokesperson. 'Ho-ho-ho yourself, Father Christmas, we're the O'Mara family.'

'The Waltons,' whispered Aisling, and Roisin choked out, 'G'night John-boy.' They erupted in giggles and Maureen shot them both a death stare.

'My son, Patrick here, has just returned home from Los Angeles with his girlfriend, Cindy.'

'Just for the week, Mammy,' Patrick was quick to interject lest she get any ideas and Cindy waved at the snowy-bearded man enthusiastically announcing in a breathy voice, 'I love Christmas.'

Father Christmas's eyes nearly popped out of his head as her bosom bounced along with her hand.

'It's the best present a mammy could have, so it is, having all her children around her and I want to capture the moment for prosterior.'

'Posterity, Mammy,' Patrick corrected her.

'And what a fine-looking family you are too in your matching tops and trousers.' Father Christmas's twinkly currant eyes were still firmly fastened on Cindy's chest.

'Aul perv, I'm not sitting on his knee,' Moira whispered.

Maureen carried on, 'Now then, I've a picture in my mind as to how I want my photograph to look.' She hustled Santa's helper out the way as she pulled Noah over to sit up on Father Christmas's knee. 'Upsy daisy, there you go, you perch yourself up there, Noah.'

Desperate to get home and get out of his sweater, Noah clambered up onto the solid red knee and began reeling off a list of things he'd like to find in his stocking on Christmas morning. Father Christmas's eyes never budged from where they'd lodged on Cindy's bosom as he nodded and muttered, 'Well now, you must have been a good boy.'

'Patrick, Cindy,' Maureen ordered, 'I want you two to stand behind Mr Claus on either side with your hands resting on his shoulder, like he's an old pal. Off you go.'

Maureen kept an eagle eye on her son and his girlfriend as they arranged themselves, before huffing, 'No, Cindy, stand up straight, shoulders back, you're not doing a Marilyn Monroe. Cop on to yourself.'

Fair play, Roisin thought. Cindy had leaned over Father Christmas's shoulder, pouting, and while Father Christmas was all for the Marilyn pose, it wasn't the stuff of the family portrait. Noah was supposed to be Father Christmas's focal point and the poor love was trying to tell him about Mr Nibbles but Cindy's cleavage was getting in the way.

Satisfied she now had Cindy in a suitably chaste pose, Maureen pointed to Roisin, Aisling and Moira, 'Right you three, you're on.'

'It's like being in a stage musical, so it is. She'll be telling us to break a leg next,' Aisling muttered as she was instructed to kneel beside the chair, hands clasped and resting on her lap, Roisin was next to her.

'Moira, you're on the other side, same pose please.'

Moira rolled her eyes but did as she was told, while Roisin looked at her mammy wondering where she was going to sit. A thought occurred to her, ah Jaysus, she wasn't going to perch herself on his other knee, was she?

'And I'm going to kneel next to Moira. Patrick I might need some help getting up again.' Maureen smiled at Santa's helper. 'I think that's us.'

Roisin half expected the girl to say, 'Thank feck for that.' She was a professional though, and assuming her position behind the tripod she said, 'On the count of three, say cheese. One, two, three...'

'Cheese!'

There was a satisfying click and the family was herded from the grotto by the helper lass. They stood blinking in the bright light of the store. The photograph wouldn't be ready to collect for another ten minutes or so, and Patrick and Cindy announced they were off to tackle the crowds and finish their Christmas shopping. Moira, Aisling and Roisin planned on doing the same, once they'd seen the photograph, and Noah was to go home with his nana, who'd another bracing pier walk with Pooh planned.

'I'm going to have a look around while we wait,' Roisin said, ensuring her son's hand was held firmly by his nana before moving away from the milling mammies and children waiting to meet Father Christmas, in order to browse the book aisles. She could see a small gathering by a stand at the other end of the store and, curious, she moseyed closer as she realised a book signing was underway. A poster behind the table at which the author sat revealed it to be for the book she'd read the review of in the paper yesterday, When We Were Brave.

The author Cliona Whelan had silvered hair, pulled back in a loose bun. Stray tendrils escaped to frame her face, which was animated as she chatted to a woman around the same age as her. She had the face of a storyteller, Roisin decided, and she was what Mammy would describe as a handsome woman with inquisitive grey eyes framed by tortoiseshell glasses. She was dressed in a crisp white dress shirt with a jauntily-tied scarf in the same shade of grey as her eyes. Roisin couldn't see what she was wearing on her bottom half as she was hidden by the table she sat at, but she was guessing it would be tailored pants. The type with little pleated nips and tucks around the waistband. Her style gave her the manner of someone direct, someone you didn't pussyfoot around, someone used to moving in a male dominated world. She had been a journalist after all. Her pen was poised, ready to sign the book the woman she was talking to had thrust in front of her.

The queue was nothing like the one she'd just endured and it was a grand opportunity to get the gift she planned on buying for Aisling personalised, Roisin decided. She sidled up to the stand of books next to the table and took one from it, handing it to the girl who was working the till at the end of the table before joining the line.

'Hello.' Cliona greeted Roisin with a smile that must have been getting tired around the edges. 'Have you a special message in mind?' Her pen was poised over the book.

'Hello,' Roisin was suddenly shy. It wasn't every day she was face to face with an author whose book was storming the charts. 'Erm could you say, Dear Aisling—' she went blank.

'How about, "Dear Aisling, I hope you enjoy this book?"'

'Grand.'

Cliona signed her sentiment with flourish and Roisin remembered her manners, thanking her and wishing her a Merry Christmas before sliding the book back in the paper bag. She put it in her bag and looking around for the others, decided the photo should be ready by now.

She found them at the main counter. The picture was being placed inside a festive red, cardboard wallet which Maureen took from the young girl with her Santa hat who was in charge of the developing. 'C'mon, Mammy, let's go outside to look at it. I'm desperate for some fresh air,' Moira said linking her arm through her mammy's and herding her toward the exit. Aisling, Roisin and Noah pushed their way out after them.

They all took grateful gulps of the carbon monoxide filled air on O'Connell Street and clustered around Maureen under the awning of a nearby shop. Noah clung to his nana's leg, tired and fed up, as she eked out the drama by pretending to be interested in the Christmas message on the cardboard wallet.

'Get on with it, Mammy. Put us out of our misery,' Roisin urged, mindful of her son who'd obviously had enough.

Maureen opened it and inspected the glossy print. Her face was unreadable as the sisters craned to see for themselves but Maureen snapped it shut before they could get a look, muttering, 'Sweet Mother of Divine.'

'Let me see,' Moira snatched at it but Maureen held it out of reach, shaking her head so her dark hair swished back and forth, her face a picture of misery.

'No.' She played the guilt card. 'All I wanted was a family photograph. A memento to pull out on those long afternoons when you've all gone back to your busy lives. Something to proudly show off to my friends. Was that so much to ask?'

Roisin draped her arm around her mammy's shoulder and gave it a squeeze. 'No, of course it wasn't, Mammy, and it can't be that bad.'

'It's going in the bin as soon as we get home, so it is.'

'Ah no, not after what we went through to get it taken. C'mon now, Mammy, let us have a look,' Aisling said. They were burning with curiosity but Maureen was not going to be swayed easily and she unzipped her handbag making to put it away, sniffing all the while.

'We'll treat you to tea at Bewley's.' Aisling knew she'd hit on a winner by bribing her mammy with a cuppa at her favourite tearooms, when she zipped her handbag up.

'Well don't expect me to pitch in,' Moira said. 'I'm a student.'

'A sticky bun, too?' Mammy eyed Aisling.

'Alright, a sticky bun too, now hand it over.' She took the wallet from Maureen, and her sisters leaned in expectantly.

She opened it and stared, in horror, at the sight of them all immortalised in their red tops and blue jeans.

'Jaysus wept, it's the fecking Addams family alright.' Moira was the first to speak, her two sisters rendered speechless as they soaked up the scene. Cindy had blatantly disobeyed Mammy's instructions and her heaving chest was resting on Father Christmas's shoulder. Patrick was staring at her assets with an expression of lust and consternation on his face. Father Christmas had obviously jumped, startled by the bosoms that had landed on his shoulder, and poor Noah was holding on to his leg for grim death like he was on a horse just off the starter blocks. Roisin's hair, thanks to the damp Dublin day, was a bushy frizz about her face—give her a top hat and she'd look like yer Slash man from Guns n Roses. Moira had her eyes shut and looked like she'd been doing the drugs while Aisling appeared to have grown a black mole on the side of her mouth. 'Why didn't any of you tell me I had a chocolate chip stuck there?'

The sisters shrugged. 'Because it was funny.'

The only one smiling beatifically at the camera was Mammy.

'And it's such a nice one of me,' Maureen lamented sadly.

Chapter 14
1957

Eighteen-year-old Cliona Whelan had never been in love before and, falling in love was the last thing on her mind as she sat on a warm, sunny patch of grass near Trinity College. A bee buzzed lazily past and the air had an autumnal tang to it she fancied she could taste. It was a curious mix of grass and damp fallen leaves. She was people watching, her favourite way in which to while away her lunch break and today was a grand day for it, given the burst of unseasonal October sunshine. On her lap was an open notebook, her scrawled shorthand filling the page as she wrote down the different characteristics of the people milling about her.

She'd been particularly fascinated by the nervous looking girl she'd seen scurry across the park, a tote bag weighed down with text books hanging from her shoulder. There'd been something about the stoop in her shoulders and the way she wouldn't meet any of her fellow students' smiles. She'd been dressed plainly in a non-descript cardigan and skirt. It was the sort of outfit that would fade from your memory moments after she faded from your line of sight. Her hair had been scraped back in a ponytail and she'd kept pushing her glasses back onto the bridge of her nose. She'd not had so much as a slick of lipstick on her face which made her look younger than she was, given she was obviously a student. There was an air of vulnerability about her as she made her way toward the college buildings, a frown firmly embedded on her forehead.

Cliona scribbled away *nervous disposition due to stress over impending exam results, probably from a small village and finding it hard to make friends in the big smoke.* She paused, pen hovering over her notebook. She needed to eat. It was lunchtime after all and if she didn't put something in her stomach, she could be sure it would make embarrassing rumblings at inopportune moments that afternoon. Accordingly, she tucked the pen behind her ear and retrieved the grease paper-wrapped sandwiches Mammy had thrust at her on her way out the door that morning.

It was a conundrum of sorts the whole falling in love thing, she mused, biting into the corned beef sandwich. She needed to experience it first-hand if she was going to write her novel, which she'd already decided would be a love story. She didn't want to use her imagination to reshape others' words. That would have felt like cheating, somehow. The thing was, most boys were scared of her. It wasn't just her height. They wanted girls in pretty frocks who agreed with everything they said. Cliona sighed.

There had been one boy brave enough to ask her out, Niall Fitzsimmons. A lanky lad who stood a whole half inch taller than her, it was enough to be respectable. He caught the same bus to Westmoreland Street as her of a morning. Niall had spent weeks positioning himself opposite her and the first time she'd caught him staring shyly at her with those dark brown eyes peering out from under his cap, she'd wondered if she had a spot or, even worse, a telltale sign she'd had egg for breakfast on her face. Then, one day he'd taken her by surprise and as she'd looked up to find him staring at her he'd asked her out in a red-faced blurt he'd clearly practised. She hadn't the heart to say no.

So, you see, it wasn't as if she was completely inexperienced when it came to romance. She'd kissed Niall at the end of their evening together too but if she were to tell the truth she'd only done so out of obligation and curiosity. He'd forked out for a fine fish supper and film. It was the least she could do. Besides, he was a nice enough lad even if he did smell of menthol and eucalyptus. That was down to the Brylcreem he styled his duck's arse with. He must go through tubs and tubs of the stuff, she'd thought, trying not to inhale as he leaned in toward her with his wet, nervous lips puckered. The feel of them as they locked on to hers like a sucker fish made her think of two things. Her father with his slicked back hair, he was a Brylcreem man, and her heavy-handed mammy wielding the Vicks VapoRub. A girl did not want to be thinking about her mammy and da, or cold remedies, when she was being kissed, thank you very much. There'd been nothing in the least poetic about it all and she hadn't gone out with him again. She suspected he caught the bus that came twenty minutes earlier as she hadn't seen him since either. She didn't have time for fellas right now, anyhow.

Cliona had decided the day the letter arrived confirming her employment at the Times that she was too practical to fall in love. Sure, what was the point? Love led to marriage and it was written right there in front of her in bold black typeface that her employment would be terminated when she married. She didn't know much about the ways of the world but she did know that it would take time to work her way up through the hierarchy to where she wanted to be. What was the point in all that steady, hard graft if just as the finish line came into sight it was all whipped away from her because she'd said, "I, do."? There was no point was the simple answer and that's why she had a plan.

She would learn the trade from the ground floor up. She would be smarter, and work harder and faster than all those other reporters with their air of self-importance as they tapped out their stories, cigarettes smouldering in the ashtrays beside their typewriters. They were always at the ready with a wise-arse answer and keen to make the girls from the typing pool blush. She would prove she was up to the job. Cliona Whelan would make sure of that. She'd become indispensable.

She thought of her mammy and her brothers and sisters. Her tribe of younger siblings were always demanding something and never very grateful for having got it. She had no desire to find herself shackled to the kitchen sink with runny-nosed little ones tugging at her apron strings crying for attention in years to come. No, she wanted to write. Writing was something she'd always done. The proof was in her diary, hidden away under her mattress, safe from her nosy, spying sisters' eyes. It was something she needed to do because it stilled the restlessness in her. How else were you supposed to get all those feelings out? Sure, Father Sheridan didn't have time to sit in his confessional box and hear her outpourings. Cliona wrote because, well because she had such a lot to say about what she saw all around her and how it made her feel.

The, world was changing, she liked to tell Mammy, and she was too modern for marriage. Sure, hadn't she got Honours in her English Leaving Certificate. She was going to be a career woman, so she was. She'd even told Mammy to stop shortening her name to Clio and under no circumstances was she to call her Clio-Cat in the presence of others. The nickname had stuck since she was in nappies and had had a fascination with pulling poor Mittens', God rest her grumpy old soul, tail. The thing was she'd said, hands on hips, as Mammy stood at the sink with her Marigolds plunged into the hot, soapy water, when she finally got to do some proper reporting—not just the rewrites and advertising editorial mind, her byline would read Cliona Whelan. Not Clio-Cat, thanks very much. It was hard enough to be taken seriously but if anyone got wind of that nickname, sure it'd be the end of her. Mammy had huffed and made an awful clattering with the plates in the sink upon hearing this and said, she was getting ideas above her station since joining the newspaper and it would be a lonely washing that had no man's shirt in it, if she continued along the way she seemed determined to go.

Clio absently pulled a piece of crust from her sandwich and tossed it onto the grass. A squalling seagull instantly swooped from where he'd been circling keeping a watchful eye on her and the other students enjoying their lunch. She didn't like crusts. something she blamed her mammy for. It was the disappointment you see. All those years of dutifully eating them and her hair still hung straight as a curtain to her shoulders. There was not so much as a kink in it, let alone a curl. Most days she pulled it back into a ponytail but once in a while, like when she'd gone out with Niall, she'd dig deep for her inner girl and coax it along with the mesh rollers, lots of backcombing and lashings of setting spray. She frowned. She'd be having words with Fidelma when she got home, so she would. She was sure she'd been helping herself to the spray. It had been three quarters full the last time she'd used it and now there was only a third left.

She watched the bird as it pranced about, sending the smaller sparrows hoping for a crumb scattering as it asserted its bullyish presence. She liked bullies even less than she liked crusts. She'd always been one to stand up for the underdog. Sure, look at the trouble she'd gotten into with Sister Evangeline when she'd told her she was being very unfair to poor Patricia Murphy. She only stuttered all the more when she was shouted at and how was the sting of the ruler being brought down on her hand supposed to help her speech? It was why she dreamed of becoming a fully-fledged journalist. She wanted to report on the injustices she saw around her. Put those bullies to rights. And then, one day, she'd publish a novel. A great sweeping, epic of a thing. Oh yes, Cliona thought, she had a plan alright.

She finished what was left of her sandwich, sweeping the crumbs from the lap of her ink-blue cigarette pants. Mammy was aghast at her insistence on wearing trousers to work, telling her it wasn't right and what would the neighbours think seeing her prance down the street bold as brass in them. Clio told her, if it was good enough for Katherine Hepburn in her heyday then it was good enough for Cliona Whelan thanks very much. How could she expect to ever have a serious assignment passed her way if she looked like a cake decoration? Besides, she'd reminded Mammy, she'd bought the pants with her own money.

Indeed, the small brown envelope she'd been handed at the end of her first week's work had been her wages. They'd burned a hole in her pocket and she'd felt ever so grown up shopping on her own. She'd come back down to earth with a bump when Mammy had greeted her at the door, eyeing her shopping bags before holding her hand out. 'You're earning now, Cliona, it's time you paid for your keep.'

A gentle breeze whipped over the green and Clio felt it tickle the downy hair on her arms. She'd rolled the sleeves of her white shirt up in order to feel the sun's kiss. The seagull was still there stalking about and so she flung the remainder of her crust in the opposite decoration, kicking her foot out at the greedy bird and telling him to shoo and give the others a chance. He squawked and flapped at her indignantly.

'What did the poor guy ever do to you?' a crisply cut American accent asked.

Clio looked up startled, her hand shielding her eyes from the sun, to see the rangy outline of a student, with a pile of text books tucked under his arms, grinning down at her. He looked to be around twenty or so and had a quiet confidence about himself as he waited for her reply. She automatically noted he was taller than she was.

'The seagull?'

He nodded and she could tell by the way his sandy-blond hair blew into his eyes, moved by the sudden gust of wind, that he didn't use Brylcreem.

'I wanted to make sure the sparrows got fed,' Cliona said, her usual bravado slipping under his gaze. His blue eyes were the colour of the marbles her little brother played with and she tried not to stare but there was something about him that made her want to keep looking.

He held out his free hand, 'I'm Gerald Byrne, but everybody calls me Gerry.'

'I'm Cliona Whelan, but everybody calls me Clio.' She was rather pleased with her comeback, even more so when she received an approving grin. She liked the way the dimples in his cheeks softened his face when he smiled and she liked the trail of freckles across the bridge of his nose, too.

'And what are you studying...?'

She filled in the gap, 'Clio, you can call me Clio.' She conveniently pushed her outburst to her mammy regarding the shortening of her name aside. Cliona suddenly seemed far too much of a mouthful, too serious all of a sudden, which was fine when it came to work but no good when you were talking to a handsome American. She half wished she'd listened to Mammy now and worn her fitted jacket and pencil skirt. She'd held it out hopefully to Clio that morning, telling her it looked a picture on her. Remembering his assumption, she replied, 'Oh, and I'm not a student.'

'What do you do then, Clio?' He eyed her notebook curiously and she snapped it shut, pinching her bottom lip between her teeth as she debated how she should describe herself. Journalist or reporter was a stretch given she spent the best part of her day typing other people's work and making tea. In the end she went with, 'I work for the Times.'

'I'm a Times man myself. I was reading this morning about that Soviet satellite, Sputnik. It's been seen over the city a second time. It's like something from a science fiction novel.'

Cliona nodded. Every newspaper in the city would have been hustling to get their story to print on time for that morning's run. 'The space race has begun.' She quoted the headline.

'Do you write for the paper?'

My, but he had a lot of questions given they were complete strangers. Cliona was unnerved. It was usually her who had all the questions. Perhaps it was just the American way of things. She liked his assumption that it was a possibility she was a journalist though, perhaps the trousers had been the right choice after all and, flattered, she told him, 'I'm a junior typist but I want to be a reporter. You have to work your way up.'

'Do you enjoy it?'

'I love it,' she replied simply. 'There's always something happening.' The clacking of typewriter keys, the shuffling of papers, telephones ringing, reporters anxiously pacing, and best of all the buzz of a big story about to break. It filled her days with excitement and anticipation. It was a long way from the typing pool to being out in the field breaking your teeth on a meaty story though. 'You're at Trinity?' She gestured to the books he was carrying.

'Yup. Third year law student on exchange from Boston Law College. My great-grandparents were both from Dublin.' He shrugged. 'Most of Boston's from somewhere in Ireland. My folks thought it was high time I came back to the motherland and saw the place for myself.' He hesitated and then asked, 'Do you mind if I join you?'

She looked him over, this confident, good-looking boy from Boston and found herself telling him she didn't mind, she'd have to go in ten minutes or so anyway. Sure, what was the harm? He sat down, his legs stretched out in front of him as he leaned his head back, raising his face to the sun and closing his eyes for a fleeting moment. 'Those rays are good. I think the whole city is outside enjoying the weather.' He gestured around him at the busy slip of green. 'Or at least the entire college.'

'That's the Irish for you. We turn into basking African meerkats at the slightest hint of sunshine.'

He laughed. 'Wow, that's some analogy.'

'I saw a photograph of them in a book once, all of them with their heads pointing up at the sun. I've never forgotten it.'

'What were you writing in there? If you don't mind me asking?' He pointed to her notebook.

'I collect character descriptions.'

He looked puzzled.

'I write down things about people that stand out or catch my eye.'

'Uh-huh, but why?'

'Because I want to write a novel one day and I figured that it would be good to have something to call on when I describe my characters.'

'So, it's a reference book?'

'Yes, I suppose it is.'

'You've a pen behind your ear, did you know that?' There was a cheeky glint in the blue irises.

She pulled it down and opened her notebook making an entry.

'Is that shorthand?'

Cliona nodded.

'What does it say?'

'A Bostonian law student with intelligent, deep-set blue eyes and twin dimples. Hair a curious mix somewhere between blond and brown. A looming, athletic build. Wearing brown trousers and a green sweater and carrying a clutch of text books. An air of insatiable curiosity about him.'

Gerry looked taken aback momentarily and this time when he threw his head back it was to laugh. Clio grinned and snapped her book shut.

'Look over there,' he said once he'd sobered. She followed the direction of where he'd pointed and saw a young woman with the most unusual shade of red hair. She stood out from the crowd, not just because she was pretty, but because of the confidence with which she moved and Cliona felt something stir. A kernel of something unpleasant knotted in her stomach, an unfamiliar feeling and she didn't like it. Nor did she under-stand why, his pointing out a good-looking girl, should make her react that way. Why did she suddenly want to be pretty and feminine like that girl? Her looks had never mattered all that much to her. You were given what you were given and there wasn't much you could do about it, so you might as well make the most of it and get on with things. She was glad for the most part that she wasn't a great beauty. To be beautiful would be a distraction from what she had to say.

She wasn't unattractive. According to Mammy's women's magazine she had a heart-shaped face and she'd been blessed with clear skin, bright inquisitive grey eyes and a nose that could have been a little smaller but one that was passable. Her nan had sighed over her waist just the other day, saying she could remember when she'd had a waist you could fit her hands around like Clio's. It was hard to imagine Nan ever being small, she'd always had a middle like a sack of spuds, but eight chil-dren would do that to you, and there was another good reason not to fall in love, and get married.

'Hair the colour of autumn fire, skin like milk,' Gerry be-gan.

Clio snapped her notebook shut and got up, annoyance pricking. So much for him being different. 'I've got to go.' She really did have to go, she only had five minutes to get back behind her typewriter. She remembered her manners. 'It was nice talking to you, Gerry.' And then, without looking back, she strode off unaware of his admiring gaze as he watched her wind her way through the various basking bodies to the street.

Chapter 15

Roisin drove down the unfamiliar treelined street Jenny now lived on, keeping an eye out for the numbers. It was a far cry from the one-bedroomed apartment on the Quays she'd once swanned about in, where Roisin had dossed down on her lumpy old sofa many times after a night on the lash. Her hands tapped the steering wheel enjoying the poppy beat of the music playing. It was a treat being out and about on her own. No Noah chattering incessantly about Mr Nibbles or Mammy pointing out what every other driver on the road was doing wrong. The first thing she'd done after adjusting the rear view and side mirrors had been to change the radio station. Mammy liked a talky-talky one because she enjoyed arguing with the host even though he couldn't hear her. She slowed a little and peered over to the left looking for a house number. 'Twenty-three,' she said out loud, 'twenty-five. Nearly there.'

She'd been sitting in Bewley's with Mammy and her sisters yesterday afternoon with a well-earned cup of tea and sticky bun in front of her—they'd all opted for sticky buns needing the sugar hit after the Christmas photo debacle. She needed sustenance too for braving the shops if she was going to finish her shopping. The air in the popular café was thick with the scent of brewing coffee and that peculiar easy-going joviality that the winding down into the festive season brought. Mammy kept opening the cardboard wallet for another look at the photo, saying that it was growing on her. Roisin suspected that was only because it was ever such a nice one of herself. She'd reached across the table to brave another glance, then wished she hadn't. The state of her. The state of them all. She couldn't be meeting Shay with a head of hair on her like that. Moira kept humming *November Rain* and she was going to put the boot in under the table if she wasn't careful. There was nothing else for it, she'd have to see if Jenny could tidy her up before tomorrow night and, rummaging around in her handbag to retrieve her mobile, she looked up her old hairdressing pal's number.

Her friend's harried voice answered a few rings later. 'It's nice to hear from you Roisin and I'm sorry your split-ends have gotten so bad, but I'm very busy, so I am. There's the twins and we've Eoin's mam and da arriving the day after tomorrow and the house is in a state, and you know what that witch of a woman is like when it comes to inspecting my skirting boards for dust,' Jenny had garbled upon hearing Roisin's request.

Roisin held her mobile away from her ear grimacing as an ear-piercing and ongoing squealing sounded in the background. She'd forgotten what the terrible twos were like and Jenny had a double dose going on.

'Don't be playing fire engines when Mammy's on the phone,' Jenny chided. 'Oscar loves making the siren noise so he does, and it's doing my head in. Jaysus now Ophelia is after being an ambulance coming to the scene. Hang on a sec would ya and I'll go in the toilet. It's the only room with a lock where I can get some peace.'

Roisin busied herself with her bun waiting for Jenny to come back on the line and when she did her voice was echoey. She hoped she wouldn't hear any other sounds while they chatted. 'As I was saying, Rosi, I'm very busy. How long are you back for because I might be able to fit you in come the new year? How does that sound, we could have a good catch up then too?'

Roisin picked up a clump of hair and eyed the ends. She wouldn't be fobbed off, not when it was imperative she look her best. She inspected her nails. Would she have time to get them done? No probably not. She'd ask Moira, she was good at manicures and Aisling would let her borrow a pair of her heels and give her some wardrobe advice. All of that was a waste of time though if her crowning glory made her look like she should be playing bass in a hard rock band. She really didn't like to do a Mammy and waltz on down the guilt-tripping road but sometimes needs must. 'Pooh's gotten very big so he has.' She aimed her dart hoping to hit the bull's eye.

Jenny cleared her throat in what Roisin decided was a nervous manner. 'I was just about to ask you how your mammy and him were getting on? It was ever so good of you to take him off our hands, like. The twins missed him for about five minutes and then forgot we ever had a puppy. Thank God.'

'Well, I was glad to help because that's what friends do and he's settled in well with Mammy. Although, it's looking like she'll be leaving her worldly goods to him, he's the apple of her eye, so he is. I have to say it was a shock to her, to all of us to realise he wasn't going to be one of your tiny lap doggy poodles like I thought, though. Sure, I wouldn't have offered to take him off your hands if it had been made clear.' She waited and when she heard Jenny's heavy sigh, she knew she'd won.

She gave Aisling who was eavesdropping across the table the thumbs up as Jenny said, 'Alright then, seeing as it's you. I can sort you out at ten but, Roisin, don't be late, I mean it.

I've to get to the shops in the afternoon or I'll have no food in for the Christmas dinner and shopping with the twins is harder than coordinating the Queen's fecking daily planner.'

Roisin smiled at the analogy. She was looking forward to seeing the gruesome twosome as their mammy called them. She slowed and indicated before turning into the driveway of 109. A tricycle lay abandoned in the front garden of the two-storey brick semi, and the flowerbeds either side of the front door could have done with a winter prune back, she noticed, getting out of her car and making her way up the front steps.

She hardly recognised Jenny when she opened the door. Where was the glamorous girl who'd had a penchant for silver jewellery and very cool clothes, more often than not in black? She'd always said black showcased whatever colour she'd put through her hair that month. The woman in front of her, whose hair was a bleached crop, looked tired as she glanced down at the jammy hand print on her oversized sweat top. She was wearing leggings and fluffy slippers that reminded Roisin of a pair she recalled her nana living in during her later years. In her hand was a mascara wand which she waved liked a traffic baton ushering Roisin in. Once the door was shut, she was wrapped in a hello hug, although she didn't squeeze back too tightly not wanting the jam to rub off on her. She knew wearing cream to visit her friend had been a bad idea but she'd wanted to go neutral after all that red yesterday.

'You're looking well on it, Jenny,' she lied. She wanted a decent haircut after all and she'd her fingers crossed for a freebie. 'Motherhood obviously agrees with you.'

'Liar.' She rustled up a wan smile. 'And I can see why you were desperate for a trim. I'm a mess but if you watch Ophelia and Oscar for ten minutes, I could tidy myself up and then make you beautiful.'

'Sounds like a good plan.' Roisin remembered her friend saying she was heading out shopping. She could recall going to get the groceries being an outing when Noah was small, *any* chance to get out of the house was an outing. 'I've nowhere I need to be, take your time. Now, where are they. They were babies last time I saw them.'

FAMOUS, FECKING LAST words! Roisin thought, lying on the living room floor as a scarf was wound around her leg. She already had a series of plasters decorating any exposed bits of her face and body. Ophelia was bandaging her leg for her. Her little face, almost hidden by the cloud of gorgeous, golden curls, was a picture of seriousness in her dress-up nurse's uniform. Oscar, her double apart from the short haircut, did an even more impressive version than the one she'd heard yesterday of a siren. *What was Jenny doing, having a nice soak in the bath and reading a good book? Had she sneaked out to do her shopping?*

A good half hour after she'd disappeared faster than a piece of chocolate cake at a Slimmer's World meeting, Jenny reappeared. It could have been a different woman. Roisin sat up and took stock of the transformation and the twins were rendered silent for all of ten seconds as they checked out this new version of their mammy. This was the Jenny she remembered. 'You look gorgeous.' She beamed.

'I feel amazing. Thanks a million for watching them, Rosi. It was such a treat to put my face on without giving a blow by blow account of everything I was doing.'

'It was no bother. We've had fun haven't we, you two?' Roisin said unpeeling the plaster from her eyebrow and hoping she didn't take half of it with it.

The twins nodded cherubically as their mammy flicked the television on for them and some eejits, dancing about in colours so bright they'd make your eyes bleed, filled the screen. She told them to be good while she gave Roisin a haircut and dragging a dining room chair behind her, beckoned for Roisin to follow her into the kitchen. 'I can't do a dry cut so I'll give you a shampoo and condition over the sink,' she said depositing the chair in the middle of the kitchen. The smell of fish hung faintly in the air; last night's dinner Roisin guessed as Jenny gestured at the sink. The bottles to the side were salon products, Roisin thought, recognising the labels. It would make a nice change from her supermarket duo. She picked up the folded towel, also on the worktop, and draped it around her shoulders before dutifully bending over and angling her head under the taps.

'How's the temperature?' Jenny asked, running the water.

Near scalding water trickled over Roisin's scalp and she yelped, 'Ouch, too hot.'

'What about now?'

'Jaysus, too cold.'

'Sorry, the tap's very temperamental. How's this?'

'Just right.'

She sounded like Goldilocks, Roisin thought, wincing as shampoo was rubbed into her scalp. Jenny had lost her touch because it wasn't a relaxing head massage she was after receiving and her back was killing her already from the stooping. There were a few moments of drama when shampoo got in her eye and she had to hold the towel to her eye to stem the stinging but aside from that she was smelling sweet and sitting in the chair ready to be pruned in no time.

A lot had happened since the last time she'd been in Dublin and she chattered about her life as a newly single woman, learning to stand on her own two feet and her hopes for eventually running yoga classes, as Jenny snipped away.

'I'd love to do yoga but there's never any time.'

'I could teach you a few basic moves. I managed to get Mammy doing some with me this morning.' She shuddered at the memory of her mammy in her yoga pants attempting the triangle pose. 'You could do them when the kids are napping or watching television.'

'I'd like that.'

'It really helped keep me sane when Noah was small.'

'And how is the young fella?'

'He's grand. He's after bringing his pet gerbil with him from London which didn't go down well with Mammy at first but she seems to be warming to the little chap. He is rather sweet.'

'I'm done with pets for the foreseeable future. Although we might stretch to a goldfish or something, you know, just so as they've got something to cart along to pet day when they start in the infants. Now shall I add some soft layers?'

'Soft layers it is.'

'So,' Jenny's voice took on an almost sly quality, 'is this desperate need for a haircut down to a certain fella?'

'I've only been separated a few months.'

'Don't come all holier than thou. It's me, Roisin, I know you of old. What's his name?'

'Shay. And it's only a drink we're going for.' She explained how they'd come to meet.

'Do you think you'll do the wild thing?'

'No! Sure, I hardly know the fella. And it's not a date or anything it's just a...' *What was it?*

'Don't move!' Jenny chided. 'It's a date, and hardly knowing a fella never stopped you in the past.'

'I was young and wild then.'

'Tell me about it, and I'm only asking because I live vicariously through other people's sex lives these days. Eoin and I were at it like rabbits when we first got married, we even did it on the kitchen worktop once.'

Roisin's eyes slid to the worktop and she decided that if, per chance, a cuppa and biscuit were offered after the haircut she'd decline.

'The last time we got jiggy, Oscar waltzed in right in the middle of it and Eoin had to pretend he was doing press-ups. By the time he'd finished explaining why he was doing them over Mammy neither of us were in the mood anymore. It's not funny!' she protested as Roisin laughed. 'Now with his mammy and daddy coming to stay there'll be no show of him practising his press-ups, not while they're in the room next door. He said it makes him feel peculiar knowing they're under the same roof.'

'Catholic guilt,' Roisin said knowingly. They all had it.

'It's that alright. What are you going to wear?'

Roisin shrugged, getting told off again for the sudden movement. 'I haven't a clue. Not that I have a lot of choice, just what I stuffed in my suitcase.'

'So, you'll try on everything you have with you, make a big mess, and then wear the first thing you tossed on.'

'Probably,' Roisin laughed.

'Have you done all your Christmas shopping?'

'I finished the last of it yesterday afternoon. Moira, Aisling and I tackled the shops. I was dead on my feet by the end of it.' Roisin closed her eyes for a moment recalling the elbow room only of most of the stores they'd visited. Unlike when the sales were on though and it was every man for himself, people were good natured and smiley. She'd enjoyed the atmosphere as they'd made their way down Grafton Street, pausing to listen to a group of young children singing carols. Seeing the Euros piling up in the upside-down hat in front of them she'd been tempted to go and fetch Noah back from his nana's and get him joining in on the Jingle Bells.

'Yes, thank God for catalogues. I did most of mine months ago from the comfort of my sofa. I've only the food to sort out now.'

'Aisling put her hand up to do our shop because with Quinn being in the restaurant business, he knows where all the best deals are to be found.'

'Lucky you lot. Now then, we're nearly done. Sit up straight.' She came and stood in front of Roisin pulling two bits of hair down either side of her face and comparing them. 'That's going to feel a lot better. I haven't taken much off just half an inch or so but it will get rid of those chewed up ends and the layers have gotten rid of all that bulk. Did you want a little bit taken off your fringe?'

'Just a teensy bit, please, Jenny.' She held up her thumb and index finger to demonstrate the quarter centimetre she wanted nipping off.

Snip, snip, snippity snip, 'Feck, Roisin, why did you jump!'

Roisin's eyes were bulbous with horror and Jenny who was looking horrified at what had just happened to Roisin's fringe spun around. She let out a scream that made Oscar's siren seem like a whispered sentiment. Standing in the kitchen doorway, not sure what all the fuss was about, was Ophelia. Her halo of curls, the curls Roisin had been admiring under half an hour ago were a memory. She looked like a little orphan girl whose head had been dealt with for the lice. 'Oscar and me played hairdressers,' she lisped.

Chapter 16

'I can't go out, not like this,' Roisin cried from the bathroom. 'I'm not coming out.'

'Rosi, sweetheart, it suits you. It shows off your pretty face,' Maureen shouted through the door but despite the fact she was shouting she still had that slightly high-pitched tone that told Roisin she was fibbing. 'Sure, it's the shock of a change that's all. Remember me with my braids? The way you all carried on? Well, that was just because you weren't used to it. A fringe like yours is what we would have called the gamin look in my day. You know like your woman, Audrey Hepburn.' Maureen paused waiting for a reply and when none was forthcoming, she urged, 'Come on out now, your sisters have just arrived. They'll sort you out. Aisling's bought cake.' She added. 'It's chocolate with a cream filling.'

Roisin was not in the least bit comforted by Mammy bringing up the Bo Derek braids she'd sported during and post her Vietnam trip. It hadn't been the change they'd all struggled with. It had been the fact that their mammy was getting about looking like an aging one-hit wonder movie star who belonged on a beach, and Howth harbour did not count. As for gamin she might as well have said gamey. She heard frantic whispering on the other side of the door as her sisters and Mammy compared notes. It seemed Mammy had brought out the big guns, insisting Moira and Aisling drop everything to come around and try and bribe Roisin from the bathroom with cake. Well, she was definitely not coming out now.

Roisin stared in the mirror. She'd tried wetting the bangs and smoothing them straight to try and add length but like a tennis ball they bounced right on up again to sit smack back in the middle of her forehead. She looked, what did she look like? She bit her bottom lip as it came to her. She looked not quite right for want of a different turn of phrase. Bloody, Jenny! She'd had to keep snipping at it until it was even after she'd slipped with the scissors. As for the twins, they'd found the discarded pair of nail scissors Oscar had used for his haircutting debut having pilfered them from the bathroom drawer, under the sofa. It had taken Roisin ages to calm Jenny down over Ophelia's new look. 'It'll grow back in no time,' she'd soothed. 'And at least it's winter and you can put a hat on her when you go out.'

They'd had to swap roles once Roisin caught sight of her crowning glory with Jenny tossing her own words back at her. 'But I'm meeting Shay tonight, I don't have time to wait for it to fecking well grow back! And I don't suit bloody hats,' she'd wailed. Jenny had followed her to the front door apologising the whole way and wringing her hands over what Eoin would say when he got home and saw Ophelia.

Roisin had driven home feeling sure every time she stopped at the lights that the person in the car next to hers was shaking their heads and thinking 'Jaysus, would you look at the state of that, God love her.' It was ridiculous but she was bordering on hysteria, and it wasn't all down to the fringe she knew. The fringe had merely exacerbated the tension building over meeting Shay tonight. When they'd gone for coffee the last time she'd seen him it had felt relaxed, and natural, but going out for a dinner well, that fell into the formal bracket of a date didn't it? She'd make an eejit of herself, she was sure of it. Well, one thing was certain she'd thought, bursting through the door of Mammy's apartment, she'd fecking well look like one.

If she'd been looking for words of comfort from her nearest and dearest, 'Mummy! You look like Mr Nibbles,' wasn't what she was after. Mr Nibbles might be cute but she had no wish to take after him whatsoever and she did not have buck teeth and chubby cheeks. As for Mammy she hadn't had to say a word. The way she'd clapped her hand to her mouth said it all. Of course, being Mammy, she'd had to say something and when she'd finally found her voice it had come out in a squeak. 'Jenny's done you proud so she has.' The only one who failed to spot the difference or simply didn't care was Pooh, who let her know he thought she was looking just fine. She shoved him away and not trusting herself to speak took herself off to the bathroom, locking the door behind her. That had been well over an hour ago.

'Ah c'mon now, Rosi. I've bought my bag of tricks. I'll have you looking gorgeous in no time,' Moira cajoled. 'Sure, it can't be that bad.'

'It is!'

'And I've bought my black Valentino's. You know, the ones with the silver diamantes on the strap that you love,' Aisling called.

'You never let me wear those,' Moira griped.

'This isn't about you, Moira. And besides, this is a crisis, so it is. The poor girl's been butchered.'

Noah was next, 'And, Mummy, I will give you the biggest and best cuddle even though I'm getting to be a big boy.' There was a pause followed by. 'Is that what you wanted me to say, Nana? Can I have a biscuit now?'

'Shush, Noah.'

Roisin looked at her reflection, trying to be objective. Jenny had done a lovely cut on the whole, her hair was shiny and had a shampoo advertisement bounce to it now the scraggly ends were gone. Maybe she *was* being silly. Maybe it was just that she wasn't used to having such a short fringe. A new look was always a shock, that much of what Mammy had said was true. Perhaps she was looking for an excuse not to meet Shay tonight. Self-sabotaging. 'Sometimes you have to step out of your comfort zone, Roisin,' she said, a misty patch forming on the mirror. 'Roisin the Brave, remember?' If Shay was worth a pinch of salt, he wouldn't care what she looked like, he'd be interested in what she had to say tonight. She reminded herself that that was exactly what she'd found so attractive about him in the first place, good looks and sexy bod aside. It had been the way his head tilted slightly to the left when she was talking, as though he was trying to listen harder. He'd found her interesting and he'd laughed when she said something funny. He genuinely seemed to like her just for her being her.

She took a deep breath and knowing her mammy and sisters were likely pressed up against the door listening, she called, 'Back away from the door, I'm coming out.'

She heard Moira mutter something about 'Who does she think she is, a cornered criminal?'

Roisin turned the lock and flung the door open. Her sisters stared at her, eyes wide, and she saw Moira clamp her mouth shut and press her lips together tightly so as not to let the laugh bubbling in her throat escape. Aisling was digging her nails into her palms in an effort to distract herself.

'What?' Roisin demanded. 'C'mon, say your piece, the pair of you. Let's get it over with.'

'No, it's nothing,' Moira's voice cracked on the word nothing.

'Moira, behave yourself,' Maureen warned.

'Oh, Mammy, I think I have to say it or I might burst. It just keeps going around in my head.'

'No. Keep your gob shut. We've had enough drama as it is. You'll not get a piece of cake if you stir up more trouble.'

'Say what?' Roisin asked, not sure if she wanted to know but wanting to know in that way you did.

Moira moved out of Mammy's reach. 'It's that old nursery rhyme, it popped in my head as soon as I saw you. *Simple Simon met a pieman,*' she broke off in peals of laughter

'Ah, God, yes. *Going to the fair,*' Aisling snorted, 'I'm sorry, Rosi,' she choked out as her giggles erupted.

'*Says simple Simon to the pieman let me taste your ware,*' Maureen finished.

'Mammy, you're supposed to be on my side.'

'I am, but it is sort of funny, Rosi.'

Roisin looked from one to the other and felt her own mouth twitch. Ah feck it, she couldn't beat them so she might as well join them.

Chapter 17

The phone rang and Moira held up her hand, 'Don't move, your nails are only just after drying. I'll get it.'

Roisin stayed where she was on the sofa and admired the natural pink shiny hue of her nails. It was an effort to sit still though when she was such a jangly bag of nerves. She made an O shape with her mouth, her face felt strange. She wasn't used to wearing so much make-up. Moira had somehow achieved that holy grail of make-up looks. The one that said I'm not wearing hardly any make-up, I'm naturally gorgeous with dewy skin and rosy pink cheeks. A-ha fooled you! Really, I've truck-loads of the stuff plastered on.

'Hello.'

She heard her sister's voice from the kitchen. *Was it Nina to say Shay had arrived?* Roisin wanted to bite her lip but she didn't want to ruin the lipstick Moira had carefully applied with a brush. 'It's a long lasting one so it won't come off when you eat and drink. It might come off if you go in for a full-on snog though,' she'd warned.

'Oh, hi-ya, Nina.'

Ah Jaysus, it was Nina, he was here!

'I will do. Tell him she'll be down in a sec and she's looking hot to trot. She's one foxy mama!'

'Moira, shut up! Do not tell him that, Nina,' Roisin shouted.

'No, I was only joking with you. Just say she'll be down in a tick. Thanks, Nina.' Moira put the phone down and reappeared in the living room. 'Prince Charming is downstairs and your carriage is waiting.'

'So, I gathered.' Roisin got up and smoothed the skirt of the little black dress she'd borrowed from Aisling. 'Sure, I couldn't get my arse in it if I tried these days,' her sister had lamented, pulling it from her wardrobe and handing it to Roisin. 'It'll be looking smashing on you though.' She'd kept her word too, loaning her the much-coveted Valentino's telling her she expected everything to be returned to her in the same condition as it had been loaned.'

She'd shot Moira a look and Moira had been indignant. 'For the millionth time, I did not scratch your Louboutin's, Aisling.' Aisling raised an eyebrow and Moira looked shifty. 'It was microscopic.' She turned to Roisin, 'She can't let it go.'

Aisling had stuck around to see the end result of Roisin's makeover and had declared her beautiful before spraying a cloud of the bottle of Oscar de la Renta perfume Quinn had bought her and ordering her to walk through it. Roisin felt the tiny droplets of perfume land on her as Aisling proclaimed she was officially hot-date ready. The fringe, she said, gave her the look of one of those pin-up girls of old. It was in the artful pencilling in of her eyebrows and the choice of bold red lip-stick. Moira had done a fine job, she'd said, before picking up her overnight bag and heading for the door. 'Have a good time, Rosi, and don't do anything I wouldn't do.'

'I certainly won't be,' Roisin had replied.

Aisling was staying the night at Quinn's and Roisin planned on sleeping in her old room. Patrick and Cindy were having dinner with Noah and Mammy in Howth and would stay the night there. She was glad Noah was with his nana because he'd have a lovely time with her and it would give him the chance to get to know his uncle and Cindy a little better. Mostly though it was because whatever tonight with Shay was, Noah didn't need to be privy to any of it.

'Right then,' she said, picking up her purse. She was keen to rid herself of the nervous anticipation that was making her body tingle. 'I'll be off. Thanks, Moira, for everything.'

'My pleasure, but before you go, one quick question. Are you all erm, you know? Spruced up.'

Roisin looked up from where she was checking her purse for her phone and key to the apartment for the tenth time since she'd finished getting ready. 'No, I don't know, what do you mean? This is as spruced as it gets. And I thought you and Ash said I looked good.'

'You do, I did a grand job, if I do say so myself but it's your bits I'm talking about. Are they in shipshape, presentable order?' Moira cast a meaningful downward glance.

'Moira! For fecks sake.'

'Ah, don't be such a prude. It's your best interests I've got at heart. It's just I know it's been a while and I'm checking it's not the Amazon rainforest down there. You know in case you lose control of yourself and jump his bones. I could stall him if you need to go and have a quick sort out.'

'Thank you for your concern, Moira, but I'm perfectly respectable down yonder, not that it matters because last time I checked you don't drop your knickers and flash your bits when you're out for dinner. Because, that's all it is, dinner!' Her voice went up a notch and Moira held up a placatory hand.

'Alright, if you say so. Don't get your knickers in a knot. Now come on let's get you downstairs.'

'You're not coming.'

'I didn't give you an hour of my life not to watch your man's reaction when he sees you.'

'Stay right where you are,' Roisin ordered, her eyes narrowed.

Moira hesitated.

'I mean it.'

Moira looked at her oldest sister's face and knew she meant business. Reluctantly she picked up the television remote and flopped down on the sofa.

Satisfied she wasn't going to be followed, Roisin closed the apartment door behind her and, taking hold of the rail, made her way down the stairs. It was a while since she'd stepped out in heels this high and she didn't want to greet Shay by tumbling down the stairs and rolling into the reception area! She reached the first-floor landing and heard a squeak on the floorboards on the landing above her. 'Moira, I know you're there, feck off with yer!'

She waited a beat and heard the footsteps backtracking, shaking her head before carrying on down. The light from the foyer was a welcoming glow as she safely descended the last flight, blinking as she emerged into it. Her stomach flipped and flopped like a thrashing fish on a hook at the sight of him. She wondered if dinner was going to be a waste of time because she wasn't going to be able to eat a thing the way she felt at that moment. It had crossed her mind as she'd waited for the minutes to tick by upstairs that perhaps she'd built Shay up into this demi-God and that when she saw him, she'd be disappointed to find he was only human and a fairly average one at that. It wasn't the case.

He was leaning against the reception desk chatting to Nina. His dark but not quite black hair was long enough to curl at the collar of his jacket. It was brown leather and she felt the urge to rest her face against it and inhale its battered smell. He had a white T-shirt on and blue jeans worn with boots. They were cowboy boots and she was reminded of her romance book cover fantasy. It was a look he wore well. He registered her presence and she remembered to close her mouth. Appreciation flickered in his eyes and she lost herself in those dark pools. He grinned, breaking the spell and she blinked as he produced a posy of vibrant blooms from behind his back. 'These are for you. You look lovely by the way.'

Roisin smiled shyly. She wanted to pinch herself, this beautiful man had brought her flowers! 'Thank you, they're gorgeous,' she managed to say, holding out her hand and hoping he wouldn't notice her faint tremor as she took the flowers and hid her face for a moment. She inhaled their sweet aroma, grateful for the chance to compose herself.

'I can put them in water for you, Roisin,' Nina offered.

'Thanks, Nina, that would be grand.'

'Have a lovely evening.' Her face was wistful.

'We will do.'

'It was nice talking to you, Nina,' Shay said, before turning his attention to Roisin. 'I've booked a table at La Bamba. I hope you like Mexican food.'

She'd eat a bowl of tripe if it meant sitting opposite him and gazing upon his gorgeousness for an entire evening.

'I love Mexican.'

Chapter 18

The Mariachi band were playing in the corner of the restaurant and Roisin sipped her beer, enjoying the traditional sounds that would make the stoniest of faces crack a smile. It was happy music, she thought, admiring their sombreros and charro outfits. A waft of cigarette smoke tickled her nose as the door opened to the balcony and a man went out to join the couple who were braving the cold in order to puff away. The restaurant was buzzing with bonhomie and shouts of laughter sounded sporadically from the group seated near her and Shay. They looked like they'd come straight from the office for a spontaneous pre-Christmas dinner. Roisin glanced over and wondered if any of them would wake up tomorrow red-faced, having gotten too friendly with a colleague after one too many slammers!

She hadn't been sure what to order to drink but Shay had said the only thing that would cool down the jalapenos and chilis in the bowl of chili she'd ordered was a Steinlager and so she'd ordered a bottle of the beer. The fluttering anxiety she'd felt earlier had dissipated, helped by the pre-dinner tequila shots at the bar and she forgot she was exceedingly out of practice when it came to having dinner with men she barely knew. He was easy to talk to. There was an openness to him that invited her to tell him about herself and over their shared entrée of corn chips and guacamole, she had. He'd done that thing, tilting his head just enough to let enough her know he wanted to hear what she had to say. He made her feel witty and interesting and when the waiter arrived with two bowls of steaming chili con carne he'd been in stitches over her description of Noah's informative chat with the Customs man about Mr Nibbles.

She inhaled the warm, spiced aroma and stirred the puddle of sour cream in as Shay told her what his plans were for Christmas.

'Mam, Philip and I are going down to Castlebeg on Christmas Eve. It will be strange to wake up on Christmas morning in the cottage where Mam grew up but special, too.'

Roisin nodded. She knew the story of how his granddad and mammy had not spoken after he'd told her to leave his house as a pregnant teenager. It was only when Shay acted as the olive branch between them that they'd made a fresh start.

'How's Reggie, doing?'

'It will be his last Christmas.' A shadow crossed his face and Roisin reached across the table without thinking to place her hand on top of his.

'I'm sorry to hear that.'

He shrugged, and she moved her hand away hoping she'd not been forward. 'It would have been nice if we could have had him for longer but, you know, at least I've had the chance to get to know him and Mam and him have put things right between themselves. He told me he can go to his grave happy, knowing everything turned out well for her.'

'It's never too late for second chances,' Roisin murmured with a sad smile, thinking of her own dad's passing. It had been hard to see someone you love wither until there was no light left inside him, but he'd known he was loved and there had to be something to be said for that—a comfort to be found in having those that loved you best in the world there with you when your time came.

'Exactly.'

They smiled at each other in mutual understanding and a current flickered between them. It unsettled Roisin and she looked away, scooping up a mouthful of her chili.

'Jaysus!' She flapped her hand in front of her mouth and Shay slid the water across the table. She gulped at it gratefully, hoping her face hadn't turned the colour of the chili she'd just been assaulted by. She could feel the beads of sweat popping on her forehead and wished with all her might she'd asked for flipping nachos and not chili. *She must look like such a prize.* Her eyes were streaming.

'Are you okay?'

'I will be,' she rasped, wondering how she'd get the rest of her meal down her without looking like she'd just emerged from a Swedish sauna.

Somehow, she managed it. The key, Roisin told herself, was little mouthfuls washed down with plenty of beer. Shay who wasn't bothered in the slightest by the heat was telling her about the festival he'd organised in Cancun on Mexico's Yucatan peninsula a few years back. It had cemented his love of the food. The hotter and spicier the better! His life, she thought, listening to his funny stories about some of the prima donna musos he'd encountered through his work as a creative producer, was fun. How many people got to do what they loved for a living? She watched his animated expression, feeling inspired.

'I want to open a yoga school, and one day I'd like to visit India,' she blurted, not knowing if the sudden revelation of her hopes and dreams was down to the beer, or whether hearing him speak with so much enthusiasm about what he did for a crust, made her want to inform him that she didn't plan on being a not very good secretary forever.

'Really?'

She nodded. 'I'm doing my training for my teaching certificate but I'll need a bit behind me before I can set up on my own. I'll get there though. I love it. Yoga makes me feel whole and I want to help other people feel like that too. When life gets tough, it's an outlet for the soul.' She might be waxing a bit too lyrically with that last bit, she thought, but it was too late to take it back and she thought she saw a spark of amusement in his eyes.

'I've never tried it but I'd like to. Things can sail close to the wind in my business and it would be good to have a stress outlet other than the pub.'

'I could show you some of the basic positions and some simple breathing exercises. They really do help to calm and focus the mind.' *Oh lordy, she had some positions she'd like to show him alright.*

'Yeah, I'd like that, thanks, and you know I don't know you all that well, Roisin, but you strike me as the sorta woman who, once she sets her mind to something, can achieve anything. I think you'll have that school of yours up and running sooner than you think.'

Oh, how she wished Mammy and her sisters were here right now to hear him say that. Actually she didn't but nobody had ever seen her as a kind of warrior woman before and she liked it. She liked it a lot.

'Another beer?'

'Yes, please.' She felt like living a little dangerously.

She decided against dessert, opting instead for a tequila sunrise from the cocktail menu. Shay went for a margarita. It had been a long time since she'd had a night out. There wasn't much in the way of spare cash for hitting the nightspots in her London life and, truth be told she didn't want to. Shay made her feel carefree, like the girl she used to be. She tossed her head back and laughed at the tale of a well-known heavy metal performer's toddler-like meltdown upon finding the wrong brand of Earl Grey teabags had been put in his dressing room.

'You've ruined him for me forever now. What happened to hard living?'

Shay wasn't apologetic.

Nature called and Roisin excused herself, getting up and making her way over to the ladies. She fanned her face, it was hot in here and her legs felt a little unsteady, but then that's what you got when you wore strappy six-inch heels. It was as she was washing her hands that she looked in the mirror and gave a small yelp at the reflection staring back at her. Christ on a bike, she'd forgotten all about the fringe. She didn't think she'd ever get used to it, or by the time she had it would have grown back to a respectable length. Still, she thought, drying her hands, Shay hadn't done that thing where he kept glancing up at it and then, realising he was staring, made himself look away. Colin had been a right gem for doing that. She never needed to look in the mirror to know she had a spot, not when Colin was on the scene.

She'd have liked to have splashed cold water on her face but didn't want to ruin Moira's efforts, besides she thought, with one last glance in the mirror, it'd be her luck the mascara she'd used wouldn't be waterproof and she'd re-emerge looking like Alice Cooper. The buzz of the restaurant washed over her as she opened the door to the Ladies and weaving her way back to their table, she saw a woman was crouching down at their table chatting animatedly with Shay. She immediately took in the fact she looked to be in her early twenties, a lithely-framed model type, all cheekbones and peachy skin. The sort of woman whose hair did what it was supposed to effortlessly, and whose fringe would never be too short.

Looking at her, Roisin suddenly felt all wrong. She was nearly thirty-seven, a mother and a soon-to-be divorcee. Who was she kidding? What was she doing here? Shay was in his late twenties and lived the kind of drifting lifestyle that didn't loan itself to fitting in with her regimented life in London. So, what was this? Why was she here? Deep breaths, Roisin, she told herself, practising the exercises she'd been telling Shay about a few minutes earlier. She approached the table with a smile firmly attached to her face.

'Roisin, this is Estelle,' Shay said as she sat back down.

She would be called Estelle. It had been too much to hope for a good old Geraldine or the likes, Roisin took the girl's soft, dainty hand and managed to refrain from giving it a hard squeeze. 'Hi, lovely to meet you,' she said in a breathy voice and Roisin instantly felt mean. Her face was open and honest as she smiled at her. Even so, Roisin was pleased to note that she had lipstick on her teeth.

'You, too.'

'Estelle and I go way back,' Shay explained. 'We met when I was just starting out.'

'At a gig in Galway.' Estelle filled in the blanks.

God, what was she then, twelve? Stop it, Roisin.

'I was dating Lex from Bad Noise,' Estelle grimaced. 'God, he was a nightmare. It took him longer to do his hair than me and he was forever pinching my smoothing serum.'

Roisin smiled despite herself at the mental picture invoked and the girl beamed back straightening up. Roisin was glad she was sitting down. Her head would have only come up to the girl's chest and as for her legs, well, they'd finish at Estelle's kneecaps.

'Well, Roisin, it was lovely to meet you and Shay.' She leaned in and kissed him on the cheek. 'Always fabulous to see you but I'll have to love you and leave you, Maxim is like a spoiled baby when he's not getting attention.' She giggled and pointed to her date who looked like a Calvin Klein advertisement as he pouted around the restaurant, a moody vision in denim.

'Yeah, you too, say hi to Bella, Sebastian and the gang for me when you catch up next. It's been way too long.'

Roisin looked at him and back at Estelle and felt like the square peg who'd never fit into the round hole world, they moved in. She knocked back her sunrise and ordered another.

Chapter 19
1957

'Nice flowers kid,' Dermot Muldoon said, gum snapping as he passed by her desk. She'd put the bouquet in an emptied-out pencil holder and was almost hidden behind the colourful blooms as she attacked her typewriter in an effort to catch up on the pile of rewrites dumped in her in-tray. The gum chewing usually annoyed Clio, they weren't Americans and Dermot loved to play the hardened, New York reporter type, modelled no doubt after films he'd seen. Today however, the thought of America and anything to do with the country made her feel like singing. In fact, she'd just had a tap on the shoulder from Ciara, who sat at the desk behind her, asking her to stop humming *Loving You*. She hadn't known she was but Ciara said she'd inadvertently typed Elvis Presley into the editorial she was working on.

Nobody had ever given her flowers before and this posy had been brought to her desk by a young delivery boy who'd winked at her and said, 'Somebody must be sweet on you.'. It had made her feel all warm inside and she knew her face had coloured. She'd been centre of attention as the other girls in the typing pool had speculated as to who her admirer was. Clio had been coy, although she'd enjoyed all the fuss. She'd ignored the whispered remark bitchy Brigid, who wore her skirts just a little too tight, had made about there being no accounting for taste.

She was only jealous, she told herself. All that mincing around the office she did was getting her nowhere.

The note she'd pulled from the envelope attached to the blooms was from Gerry. There was no one else they could have been from and her pulse beat a little quicker at the thought of him thinking enough of her to splurge on a bouquet. She'd held the message close as she read it, well away from the others' prying eyes.

Dear Clio, I hope I didn't offend you the other day and if I did well, this is my way of apologizing for being a brash and insensitive American. I thoroughly enjoyed our conversation and would like to invite you to afternoon tea at that most Irish of establishments, the Merrion Hotel this Saturday at 3.30pm. I shall wait for you in the drawing room where I believe the people watching is excellent and I hope I'll see you there.

Clio gazed at the flowers, once more losing herself in the intricate patterns of the petals. Nature was a wonderous thing she thought dreamily, jumping a moment later as the chief's booming growl sounded from his office. 'Clio where are those damned rewrites? They should have been on my desk half an hour ago.' Her fingers began to fly over the keys once more. Nature was all well and good but she had a job to do, she told herself sternly.

CLIO'S WEEK WAS MERCIFULLY busy although her mind kept drifting to Saturday and what she would wear. She'd seen a dress in the window of Brown Thomas on her way to get the bus and had stopped to stare. It was lemon coloured with a nipped-in waist and full skirt and the slogan next to it said 'Be a Ray of Sunshine on an Autumn Day. Yellow looked well on her, she knew that. The dress was far prettier than anything she had hanging in her half of the wardrobe at home. She mentally poured herself into the dress and imagined the admiration in Gerry's eyes as she swept in through the hotel's doors, white gloves on and cardigan draped over her shoulders. The doorman would fall over himself to greet her and Gerry would think himself a fortunate fellow indeed. She'd blinked, aware of the people hurrying past her and feeling rather foolish standing gawping at a shop window. She reminded herself that she wasn't really a ray of sunshine on an autumn day sort of a girl. No, she'd resolved, come Saturday afternoon she would be herself because that's exactly the sort of girl she was and if he didn't like it then he wasn't the fella she hoped he might be.

Even so, she'd taken an age to get ready come Saturday. She'd fussed with the rollers and had been pleased with the way her hair curled under at the ends. As for her bouffant, for once it didn't look like a sponge pudding sat on top of her head. All in all, someone was on her side she thought, giving it a final dousing with the setting spray. She'd compromised inasmuch as she ever did by teeming her checked pants with a lemon sweater. She didn't normally bother with make-up, she was always in too much of a hurry to head out the door and find out what was happening in the world. Today however, she applied a peachy, pink lipstick before standing back from the dressing table mirror to admire her handiwork. A giggling sounded from the doorway and she spun around to see Fidelma peering around it. She made kissing noises and, as Clio lunged at her, she tore off down the hallway, her feet thundering down the stairs to the safety of her mam's skirts in the kitchen. Clio followed at a pace befitting a young woman about to go for afternoon tea at the Merrion.

'Leave your sister alone, Fidelma,' she heard Mammy admonish over the cacophonous noise coming from the kitchen. She poked her head around the door in time to see her sister's cheeky face peer around her mam to see how the land lay. A pot was bubbling on the stove, its lid rattling, and the savoury smell of stew clung to the air. The twins Tom and Neasa were banging spoons on upside down pots playing the drums and looking pleased with their musical ability. Tom was clutching a piece of cheese in his spare hand and Tabitha, Mittens' predecessor was cowering in the corner ever hopeful of a tasty titbit being sent her way.

It was a madhouse, she thought calling over top of the ruckus, 'I'll be off then, Mammy.'

'Ah now, hang on just one moment, young lady. Tom, Neasa, give that a rest, you're giving me an awful headache so you are. And Tom give me that cheese if you're not going to eat it.' Tom pressed the cheese into his mouth defiantly and Mammy sighed, turning her attention back to Clio.

'Now who is he this fellow of yours? And what is it he does?'

'Mammy!' Clio rolled her eyes. She'd already told her more than once. 'We've been through all of this.'

'Don't you Mammy me, not when you're after stepping out with a fella we've not met.'

Clio decided to tread a little more carefully. She was lucky it was just Mammy she was having to deal with, Da thanks be to God had gone to watch the match. 'His name's Gerald Byrne and he's an Irish American from Boston. He's in Dublin for the year studying at Trinity—a third-year law student.'

'A law student, and from Boston, you say.' Mammy's eyes were alight and slightly glazed. Clio knew she'd just transported herself from her kitchen in Phibsborough to a swanky Boston society wedding where she, as mother of the bride, was clad in the very latest haute couture. She'd have a hat on too, Clio mused, a great big one with feathers like one of the three musketeers knowing Mammy. She read far too many magazines for her own good.

CLIO FELT LIKE SHE'D stepped into another world as she was ushered through the doors of the elegant Georgian hotel. She paused for a moment in the foyer and fancied she could smell the stories imprinted on the Merrion's walls. The air was fragrant with extravagant floral arrangements and, to Clio's mind, there was a hushed, almost reverent atmosphere rather like being in church. The foyer was quiet this time of the day and a well-groomed young man with a pencil-thin moustache looked up from the concierge desk to ask if he could help her. 'I'm meeting a friend in the drawing room,' she explained a hand automatically going to her hair to check it was still sitting where it was supposed to be and hadn't morphed into a bird's nest on the journey here.

'Certainly, madam.' He gave a tight smile, his moustache curving upwards, and gestured to a porter asking if he would 'Show madam to the drawing room.' She hurried behind the liveried boy who didn't look much older than herself and found herself in the entrance of an understated, refined room full of intimate tables and comfortable armchairs in which several guests lounged with the casual air of people well used to the finer things life had to offer. A colossal chandelier dominated the space sending shafts of rainbow lights darting about the room. Flames spluttered and coughed from the open log fire and there, sitting in the middle of it all and looking every bit as handsome as she remembered, was Gerry.

His face lit up as he saw her, and Clio thanked the porter. She tried to stop the big goofy grin from spreading over her face as he got up to greet her. 'I wasn't sure you'd come. You look wonderful by the way.' He kissed her on the cheek and she inhaled his scent closing her eyes for the briefest of moments trying to pinpoint the familiar, fresh smells. It was Pears soap and green apple shampoo she deduced, accepting his invitation to sit down in the chair opposite him.

'Shall I order us tea and scones?'

'Grand.'

He did so and then produced a packet of Player's from his shirt pocket. He opened it and giving it a tap offered the protruding cigarette to her.

'Oh, no I don't, thanks.' She'd had a puff on the cigarette her friend, Deirdre, pinched from her mammy's apron pocket when they were thirteen. She'd thought she was going to cough up a lung and when she'd finished wheezing, she'd felt violently ill. It had put her off for good.

'Do you mind if I do?'

'No, of course not.'

She watched him from under her lashes as he lit the cigarette with a gold Zippo. It was engraved but she couldn't read what with. He saw her looking at it.

'A twenty-first present from my folks. I've a matching hip flask.'

'So, you're twenty-one.' She'd wondered.

'Closer to twenty-two and what about you, Clio, how old are you?'

'Eighteen. I'll be nineteen in June.' She watched him lift his head and exhale a plume of smoke. There was something elegant about the process and she almost wished she did smoke.

'So,' he said lazily. 'Tell me more about yourself. What makes you tick, Clio Whelan.'

'Well,' Clio thought about his question, 'I suppose what drives me is my need to break the mould.'

'What do you mean?'

'I mean, I don't want to wind up being an Agony Aunt for the paper or writing a women's lifestyle column. That isn't what I want to read when I pick up the paper. I want to read about what's going on in the city and that's what I want to report on. There aren't any women doing that and I think it will be a while before there are, but I intend to be right there with my pen and pad at the ready when things change. And I want to write my book of course.'

Gerry could see the passion in her eyes as she spoke. 'And, I think you'll do both.'

Clio checked his smile but there was no hint of condensation or indication that he might be humouring her, as was apt to happen when she put voice to her dreams. The only thing she could read in his expression was admiration.

'There's more to you than your ambition, though. What about family, you know brothers and sisters?'

'Oh,' she waved her hand dismissively, 'I've too many of both.'

Something, her words or her expression, Clio wasn't sure, made him laugh and encouraged she told him all about the Whelan madhouse.

'It sounds like fun.'

'Chaos more like. They drive me mad all of them but I love them dearly. What about yourself?' She looked at him sitting back in his chair, legs crossed, relaxed, and was struck by how at ease he was here in the hotel. Taking tea in upmarket establishments was clearly something he was used to unlike herself who was perched on the edge of her seat half expecting a tap on the shoulder from the concierge asking exactly what she, Cliona Whelan from Phibsborough was doing there. She could sense from his quiet confidence how different their lives were and the seed of an idea was planted.

'What do you want to know?'

'Everything and do you mind if I take notes?' Her hand was already closing around the notebook she never left home without.

'For your character profile?' He looked amused as he took a long drag on his cigarette.

Clio watched the tip glow brightly and the ash begin to bend. He flicked it in the ashtray and looked at her expectantly.

'No, I've an article I'd like to write.'

'About me? I can assure you, your far more interesting than me Clio.'

She shook her head. 'I disagree. Your life's so different to mine and the average Dubliner, Gerry therefore it's automatically of interest especially as so many Irish have family in Boston. I want to know about what your life there's like. Why you feel connected to Ireland even though your third generation. The, things you did growing up that sort of thing. What it means to you and your family for you to spend a year at Trinity and how it differs from college life in Boston. I'm sure others would too.'

'I think you're quite mad, Clio.' He shook his head and ground his cigarette out.

'A little maybe, but most of us Irish are.' He smiled at that and encouraged, she clicked her pen testing it on the blank page she'd opened her notebook to. 'Well, what do you say?'

'Will you let me read it when you've written it?'

'Of course.'

He studied her intently for a moment. 'I don't think you are the sort of girl who takes no for an answer are you, Clio?'

'I'm most certainly not,' she said, mock-sternly.

He grinned. 'Well then, I've no choice. Where should I start?'

'Tell me about your family and what it was like growing up in Boston.'

Clio listened intently, her hand flying across the page, not wanting to miss a word of what he was saying. She was right, his life was as different to hers as could be and reading between the lines, she sensed his family was wealthy. What they called in America, old money wealthy. Gerry was one of three boys who'd had a pretty sheltered childhood. He'd gone to good Catholic schools, summered in Cape Cod, that sort of thing.

She watched his face grow illuminated as he described the wide sky and endless stretches of sand and the sense of freedom he'd always felt arriving at the Cape, knowing the whole summer was his to lie on the warm sand, to run down the beach as the waves caught his feet, and to swim. As a teenager he'd been good at track and he'd have liked to have studied medicine. Medicine was a noble profession, he said, but as the oldest son, a career in politics was predetermined. His father moved in those circles and it was an assumption Gerry had grown up with that he would follow in his father's weighty footsteps. She detected a slight bitterness in his tone and tried to imagine having no choice over what direction you pointed your life in.

He only stopped talking when the pot of tea and a plate of scones with fresh cream and a bowl of strawberry jam arrived and were put down on the table in front of them. They dived into them and when he leaned across the table to wipe off the blob of cream she'd somehow managed to get on the tip of her nose, Clio knew she was falling in love with the good-looking American with the candid smile opposite her.

Chapter 20

Present

Clio's fingers hovered over the keys. She was in her writing room, the room that doubled as a guest room when she'd had Fidelma's children stay over through the years. Her desk overlooked the back garden, which was an unruly display of cottage garden flowers in the summertime. Clio liked the disorderly and riotous colour that ran rampant through the warmer months in her otherwise orderly world. She liked to get amongst her flowerbeds and hear the humming bees as she pulled weeds and trimmed edges. She'd found over the years that, when she was in her garden getting her hands dirty, her mind was free to roam and the scene that had been tied in knots would become untangled so that when she sat back down behind her typewriter the words flowed.

Today the lawn was covered in a blanket of snow and she watched her little friend the robin redbreast, who visited her apple tree most days. It came to nibble on the bird feeder she hung from the branch of the tree. She'd placed it safely out of reach of Bess whose arthritic old bones meant her climbing days were over. The bird's shiny black eyes fixed on something only it could see as it perched on the spindly branch. She admired its stillness and the vibrant orange, red feathers of its breast. There was a lot of folk lore associated with the bird; Clio knew the stories. To kill the robin, the tale went, would result in a tremor in the hand of the perpetrator for the rest of their days. They were messengers from the spirit world, that signalled the death of a loved one. She didn't go in for all of that, she just liked to watch the little bird's graceful, darting movements and enjoyed the splash of colour its visit brought on an otherwise dull day.

She was also glad of the distraction because since she'd received Gerry's card, the words refused to come. She'd sat down in front of her typewriter, a cup of coffee you could stand a spoon up in alongside it because she liked the mellowed rich smell. It reminded her of her days working in a newsroom and she liked to think it was the scent of industriousness. There'd been nothing industrious about her sitting at her desk staring at the window these past days though, as she found herself lost in the past. It didn't pay to look backwards when you got to her age, Clio thought. There was no point in questioning the decisions you made when you were young. What was done was done.

She sighed and got up, knowing she was going to read through the box of letters she'd tucked away in the attic years ago, and which from time to time she'd revisited over the years. There was one for every week Gerry was away from her for those three months until she'd broken things off. Love letters full of hope for the future. Mostly, Clio scanned through them, her eyes misting as she wondered how her life might have been had she gone to Boston as they'd planned. She knew he'd married from grainy newspaper copies of the Boston Globe thumbed through at the library. She knew too he was a widower and had been for some time. The knowledge he'd married had caused a bittersweet pain, especially when she'd read he'd had children too. Sons, three handsome mini versions of their father, and she wondered if the eldest would be expected to rise high in politics like his father and grandfather had before him. The shoebox was where she'd left it, downstairs on the side table next to her sofa. She'd been going through the letters again last night, enjoying the warmth from the fire as she'd travelled back in time.

Chapter 21

1958

Clio huddled inside her coat as she waited on the corner of Grafton and Dame Street for Gerry. The weather had been brutal these last few days. Winter seemed to be intent on not letting spring get so much as a look in, despite it nearly being April. She was wishing they'd arranged to meet inside a cosy pub instead of on this street corner where the wind whipped around. She watched a pile of leaves in the gutter dance about in a private whirlpool and then, looking up, spied Gerry's familiar loping gait as he strode toward her. The smile, the one she could never contain when she saw him, broke out on her face despite the fact she was on the verge of hypothermia.

'Hello, darling, you look frozen. You weren't waiting long, were you?' He kissed her with a passion that received a disapproving look from a woman marching past, whose headscarf was knotted so tightly against the wind it had given her an extra chin. He took her hands in his and tried to warm them.

'That wind cuts you in half, c'mon let's go somewhere warm,' Clio said through chattering teeth once he'd released her.

'Kehoes?' he suggested, and she nodded, not really caring where they went so long as there was a fire. She tucked in under his arm enjoying the way she fitted just right and they made their way up Grafton Street. They veered into Anne Street where they burst in through the saloon style, stained glass doors of the pub with the same gusto as the cowboys of old. Clio loved the old place. It was to the Irish literary world what Sloppy Joe's bar in Key West had been to Hemingway. Clio adored Hemingway although she admired Virginia Woolf more.

The pub, with its dark wood panels and booths, smoky atmosphere, and aroma of whiskey that somehow permeated it all, felt like a space in which a great novel would have been plotted out. Since she'd turned eighteen and had finally been old enough to frequent the city's pubs, Kehoes had become a firm favourite for its most excellent people watching. Although, she was happier sipping on a glass of lemonade than a pint of the black stuff Gerry had been so determined to enjoy. 'I can't be considered a proper Irishman if I don't drink Guinness, Clio,' he'd said.

She'd replied, 'But you're Irish American.'

'Same difference where I come from,' he'd said grinning, and she'd pointed to his foam moustache with a smile.

Now, she slid into a booth. The pub was toasty warm thanks to the fire, and a group of men who looked like they'd had a hard day's labouring were clustered at the bar, putting the world to rights over their pints. There were a few younger people, students who fancied themselves intellectual types with little round glasses perched on their noses, hair a little too long, and wearing cool, black polo necks. They wore earnest expressions as they sat deep in debate, smoking languorously with their half-finished drinks in front of them.

There were only two other women in the pub, Clio noticed. The girlfriends of the intellectuals, but it pleased her to see they were taking part in the heated debate with just as much passion as their male counterparts. She glanced at her watch. It was five o'clock. She had time for one drink and then she'd have to get off home. Not that her parents would make too much fuss were she to run a little late for dinner. They thought Gerry was the best thing since sliced bread and had high hopes of her forgetting about her career and concentrating on more important things like marrying well. Marrying into Boston society to be precise. Clio planned on having both.

She watched him ordering their drinks. It was hard to believe they'd been courting since September. Time had passed so quickly and in the last six months Gerry had become so much a part of her life she could no longer imagine herself without him beside her. A shiver passed through her. In a few weeks he would be leaving. His passage was booked across the pond to America. Him not being here in Dublin would be like... well, it would be like losing a limb, or an integral part of herself at the very least. It was a pain she didn't want to think about. All her spare time was spent with him, so much so that her mammy had warned her not to neglect her friends or she'd have none to choose from as bridesmaids. Fidelma and Neasa had been most indignant because, they'd told Mammy, it was they who should be bridesmaids. At that point Clio had held up her hand and told them that she had no idea where all this talk of bridesmaids had come from because she wasn't even engaged.

'Ah, but you keep playing your cards right, Clio, and you might just find a lovely, sparkly ring on your finger.'

'It's Cliona, Mammy,' was all Clio had dignified her mammy with by way of response.

Gerry returned with their drinks and slid into the seat opposite her. He'd no sooner settled himself and raised his pint glass to his lips when she launched into the breaking news from America. It was a story she'd typed for their World News reporter, Ed, that afternoon and one she was itching to share. The United States had launched its Vanguard 1 Satellite. 'Isn't it incredible to think of it orbiting up there?' She pointed skyward. 'They say it will be up there for two thousand years, imagine that?'

Gerry nodded his agreement but, as she opened her mouth to fill him in on the finer points of the US's latest space mission he held a hand up to silence her. 'Clio, honey, let me get a word in would you.'

'Oh, sorry.' She was contrite, and looking at Gerry's serious expression a little worried as to what it was he wanted to say. She clutched her glass a little tighter, her knuckles suddenly white. To her relief his face softened.

'Don't look so worried. It's just I think we need to talk about the future, don't you?'

Clio studied him and her mouth suddenly felt dry. She took a sip of the sweet syrupy drink in order to stall the tête-a-tête she wasn't sure she wanted to have. She didn't want to *think* about him leaving, let alone put voice to it. His steady blue-eyed gaze didn't falter from hers and finally she replied with a weighty sigh, 'Yes, I suppose we do.'

'I want you to come to Boston.'

Her eyes widened and he hurried on. 'Hear me out. I'll go back as planned and then in a month or so, when I've had a chance to talk things through with my folks and to put the arrangements in place, I want you to come over.'

Clio couldn't make sense of what he was saying and her face must have reflected this because Gerry took her hand in his and said, 'I'm not making a good job of this and I have a ring. It's my grandmother's actually but it's not here.' He stopped, his usual confidence having deserted him, his words sounding jumbled to his own ears, and took a deep, steadying breath. 'What I'm trying to say, Clio, in my ham-fisted way is, I want you to be my wife.'

Clio gave a tiny gasp as his grip on her tightened ever so slightly.

'Marry me, Clio Whelan. I've never met anyone like you before and I can't imagine my world without you in it.'

'Oh.' She blinked. She hadn't been expecting that but suddenly her mouth twitched and that big goofy grin, the one she could never contain for long when she looked at Gerry, spread across her face. 'I would love nothing more than to marry you.'

Present

Clio gazed at the letter she had clutched in her hand. It was the last correspondence she'd ever received from Gerry until the Christmas card that had arrived the other day had sent her into such a spin. Old memories seemed so fresh when they were brought out and examined like this, she mused, eying the words in that oh so familiar handwriting in front of her. Words she could almost recite by heart. The letter was dated the eighth of July 1958. Gerry had been home for three long months when she'd received it. She'd run up to her bedroom, ripping it open eagerly, as she did every Friday when his letters arrived like clockwork, and the ticket for her passage had fallen out along with a note from his mother.

It was real, it was really going to happen, she was going to Boston, she'd thought, picking the ticket up and staring at it with both fear and excitement. The note, she saw, was neatly written on embossed personalised stationery and it was intended to welcome Clio to the family. Mrs Byrne wrote how excited she and Mr Byrne were over her and Gerry's engagement. How lovely it was going to be to welcome a daughter into the family, and that they were so looking forward to meeting her. She'd expressed sympathy, understanding the idea of setting sail for a new country must be daunting both for herself and her family, but that she, and her parents were not to worry. She'd be well looked after. Arrangements had been made for the sake of propriety for her to stay with a Mrs Geraghty who was used to lodging homesick young women and would look after her well. She ran a clean and respectable establishment where Clio would stay until the wedding. After which she and Gerry would be gifted a townhouse in which to start their married life. Cliona had skimmed over the rest of the note.

We've a lot to organize, my dear, with your engagement party and the wedding. John pulled some strings and the Holy Cross Cathedral is booked for the 9th of November. It's quite the coup given the short notice. Wait until you see inside it, Cliona, my dear, it is breathtaking and the acoustics have to be heard to be believed. I get goosebumps just thinking about it all. You and Gerald will be the toast of the town! Now, given it's to be a winter wedding I'm thinking Balmain for the gown. Audrey Hepburn wore a Balmain on her wedding day and the sleeves were magnificent and perhaps, Balenciaga for your engagement? Oh, we're going to have such fun, you and I, Cliona. As for the invitations plain black ink on cream paper is simple but stylish don't you think?

The rest of the words had blurred. It was like trying to read a foreign language. She'd put the note to one side and scanned Gerry's letter, wanting to find comfort in hearing his voice through his words. It hadn't helped quell her anxiety though, as he'd written his mother was driving him nuts because all she could talk about was the engagement party and the wedding. The engagement party was intended to formally introduce Clio to Boston society and Mrs Byrne was hopeful of the Kennedys attending both. She was getting herself very agitated over the arrangements and was impatient for Clio to arrive so they could finalise the details. There was a lot to be done, or so his mother said. He'd be just as happy for them to elope but he'd never be forgiven if they did. Don't worry, my darling, he'd written. Once we're married our life will begin.

The letter and its enclosures had arrived seven days before she was due to sail, plenty of time for Clio to begin to feel apprehensive about the idea of crossing the Atlantic on her own. She wanted Mammy to come with her but she couldn't leave the littlies and 'Besides,' she'd said, 'wasn't it better they saved their pennies for the wedding? Sure, you'll be grand, Clio, aren't you a capable young woman, who's going to be welcomed into her new family. There's nothing to be anxious about.' But Clio was anxious.

Mammy and Daddy were in raptures the more they learned of what she could expect on her arrival. 'You'll never have to work again, Clio. Sure, it's a life of fine clothes and a fine home for you, my girl. You'll be living in the lap of luxury,' Mammy had trilled. She'd caught her telling Mrs Fitzpatrick two doors down that she and Gerry were being given a townhouse in Boston as a wedding present. 'Imagine that?' she'd said to the hard-faced old woman who used to tell Clio and her friends off for being boisterous when she was younger. Mrs Fitzpatrick had turned pea green. Mrs Byrne had said she and Gerry would be the toast of the town. Well, she was definitely the talk of the street, Clio had humphed to herself, because she'd also overheard Mrs Fitzpatrick telling Mrs Murphy in a voice designed to carry, that young Cliona Whelan had gotten ideas above her station.

When Mammy wasn't telling anyone who cared to listen about Clio's new life in Boston she was fretting over the Whelans showing her up. Worried they'd arrive in Boston looking like country hicks from over the sea. She'd been making cutbacks when it came to the food bill so as to deck them all out in clothes befitting a society wedding. This was to the disgruntle-ment of Clio's brothers and sisters who were sick to the back teeth of being told they'd have to behave themselves when they were in Boston. 'Why couldn't you marry someone normal?' Fidelma had whined, upon finding the strawberry jam had not been replenished.

Clio recalled her mammy asking her, on the Thursday be-fore she was due to sail, what they'd said when she'd told them she was getting married at work. She'd carried on eating her toast even though, like everything else she tried to eat of late, it tasted like cardboard. Her mammy, who had her back to her at the worktop as she strained the tea, hadn't waited for an an-swer. 'I'd have thought they might want to run a story on you. You know local girl makes good, that sort of thing. Did you tell them there's a possibility Mr and Mrs Kennedy might be at your wedding?' She turned around then and Clio had just smiled and nodded vaguely which was enough to appease her. She'd picked up her plate and rinsed it in the sink before kiss-ing her mam goodbye on the cheek and heading out to catch the bus. She'd tried not to think about it being the second to last time she'd ride this bus through the streets she knew like the back of her hand but her eyes had burned with threatened tears, nonetheless.

She hadn't said a word to anyone at the newspaper, not a word and she didn't know why. Oh, she'd tried. She'd hovered outside her boss's office and when he'd shouted at her to stop loitering and get on with her work, she'd scurried off instead of saying what needed to be said. That long-ago Thursday as she clacked away at her typewriter she'd found it hard to believe that come Monday she wouldn't be there. Her chair would be empty and all she'd be remembered for was the girl who'd skulked off to America to get married without so much as a word. Nobody would ever say, 'Cliona Whelan, she was one of the finest reporters we ever had.' So it was, she left the building at 4.30pm on the Friday afternoon as though it were just any other day. She waved to the girls from the typing pool and called back to them to enjoy the weekend before getting on her bus and going home.

The next few days had passed in a strange twilight-like fugue for her. She went through the motions of packing her case—she planned to travel lightly—and on Saturday night there'd been a farewell supper held in her honour. As her friends and family laughed, chatted and clinked glasses she'd felt as if she were standing outside herself, a stranger listening in to people talking about some girl she didn't know. Nobody noticed anything amiss with her and Clio had wished more than anything that she could sit down with Gerry, face to face, and tell him how she was feeling, but he was literally an ocean away from her.

The day itself rolled around as big occasions always do and in this new dreamlike state that had overtaken her, she'd found herself being jostled by the crowds gathering at Dublin Port, waiting to board or wave off loved ones on the Orion. The huge liner loomed over them all with its steady stream of passengers walking up the gangplank. The day was cold but it didn't touch Clio; she was unaware of the sorrow, anticipation and excitement that filled the crowded dockside. She was oblivious to the scent of the sea, salty and fishy, which made Neasa's nose curl and Tom declare the port, "stinky" which saw him get a cuff around the ear.

She was hugged and kissed and aware of Fidelma urging her to look out for her orange scarf when she stood on the deck to wave down at them; she'd worn it in order to stand out. Mammy was crying, and Daddy was stoic as he nudged her into the throng filing up the gangplank. Her case banged against her leg as she was swallowed up in the crowd, all eager to board the ship and begin their journey. She showed her ticket and passport and then followed the sea of coats and hats to the upper deck where she squeezed in between two families to scan the dock for a last glimpse at her own family's familiar faces.

An orange slash of colour split the grey day and her gaze settled on Fidelma waving frantically with her scarf. A wave of love for her sister crashed over her and she waved back, hoping she could see her. Her arm began to ache with the effort, and the stupor Clio had been in began to lift. The calls of the men working on the wharf below mingled with the excited chatter all around her became overly loud. She could smell the salt air and everything sharpened and cleared like the lens of a camera being twisted into focus. Her arm dropped to her side as it hit her what had been niggling at her since she'd received that last letter from Gerry.

If she were to marry him, she would cease to be. That girl who'd stood outside Brown Thomas admiring the yellow dress, the dress that suggested she be a ray of sunshine on an autumn day, the girl who'd been strong enough to know her own mind, would be swallowed up. Because just as she wasn't a ray of sunshine on an autumn day sort of a girl, nor was she cut out for Balenciaga or Balmain. Her life she realised, were she to travel to Boston would be immersed in Gerry's. Her job from the moment she said "I do" would be to support him, and his family's political aspirations.

She loved Gerry. She loved him with all her heart, but she knew right then that she couldn't marry him. She began to elbow her way back through from where she'd come, moving against the tide as she pushed her way back down the gangplank toward the orange scarf. She was Cliona Whelan, she told herself. The girl who would not quit until she was reporting newsworthy stories for the Times. The girl who would write a bestseller. She'd gotten sidetracked, but she'd found her way back to herself.

CLIO FOLDED THE LETTER and put it back in the box before placing the lid down firmly. She hoped by doing so she was shutting those memories in so she could get back to work. To her surprise she found her cheeks were wet and she wiped the tears away angrily. She had a book to be getting on with. She didn't have time for dwelling on ancient history. Why had Gerry decided to come back now? What could he possibly hope to have happen at their time of life? She was only a year away from getting her bus pass for God's sake.

Chapter 22

Roisin made her way down the stairs, her nose quivering like the little red fox at the smell of bacon frying. The aroma was curling its way up the stairwell from the kitchen in the basement. She clutched the bannister, feeling unsteady on her feet despite her sensible footwear. Her head was pounding and she vowed for the tenth time since she'd opened one eye earlier that morning, only to be assailed by a needle like pain in her head, she'd never touch tequila again. She hadn't had all that much to drink but she was out of practice given she hardly led the life of a party girl these days and it had gone straight to her head. The apartment was silent when she dragged herself out of bed, for which she was grateful.

She could vaguely recall Aisling having said something yesterday about taking the opportunity to head off early do a spot of Christmas shopping. There was a tour party returning from their travels later this afternoon and she'd have to be back by then. Moira, she'd deduced, was probably out with Tom making the most of the college break. She didn't want to deal with her sisters quizzing her about her night out with Shay. Come to that she didn't want to think about her night out. All she wanted was a new head. That wasn't too much to ask was it? Failing a new head then a visit see what Mrs Flaherty had on offer in the kitchen would suffice. 'A rasher sandwich will fix me up.'

'What was that, Roisin?'

Roisin started, she hadn't seen Ita, O'Mara's director of housekeeping as she insisted on being called, loitering in the doorway of Room 7, the trolley of cleaning products nowhere to be seen. Ita's phone made a telltale ding from her pocket and the younger woman looked sheepish.

'Oh, hello, Ita. I didn't see you there. I was just saying I fancy one of Mrs Flaherty's rasher sandwiches.'

'Talking to yourself is the first sign of madness, so it is.' Ita moved closer and peered at her. 'You don't look very well, Roisin.'

Roisin knew she was an unbecoming shade of green and she should have brushed her hair. She had managed to brush her teeth and get dressed, that was something at least.

The younger woman looked sly. 'Big night on the lash, was it then? Has your mammy got your lad?'

Roisin saw the gum in her mouth and felt irritated. There was just something about Ita that was annoying. It wasn't just her insufferable air of superiority, evident in the fact she seemed to think her work or more aptly lack of work at O'Maras was beneath her. Or the way she lurked about the hallways of the guesthouse not doing much of anything other than earwigging and playing on her phone. Roisin knew she drove Aisling, who was obligated to her employ her through Ita's mammy and their mammy's longstanding friendship, mad. 'Not at all, Ita, I'm grand so I am, and yes, Noah stayed overnight at his nana's along with Pat and his girlfriend Cindy.'

'Patrick's home?' Ita breathed, her pinched features taking on a moony quality. Roisin mentally rolled her eyes, she was obviously another one of her brother's many admirers.

'Yes, he's home for Christmas. Mammy's made up, so she is.' She answered as brightly as she could then, keen to get downstairs, added, 'Oh, Aisling asked me to mention if I saw you that she'd shortly be checking on the rooms that needed to be made up for the guests returning from their tour this afternoon.' She felt better watching Ita pale and scurry off. It was a little white lie but it was satisfying watching her get moving. It was about time she earned her wages!

Roisin carried on her way, reaching the ground floor without bumping into any guests, and with the smell of a good old Irish fry-up getting stronger, her mouth began to salivate. *Salvation was nigh!* She spied the back of Bronagh's head, dipped slightly as she huffed over entering the pile of faxed bookings into the computer and was relieved she was busy. She'd creep past and say hello once she had some good old greasy, soaky-uppy, sustenance inside her. She'd only got one foot on the last flight of stairs leading down to the basement when Bronagh's voice rang out.

'Roisin, don't try and sneak past without telling me how your night went with the handsome Shay. I've eyes in the back of my head so I have and I've been waiting for you to make an appearance. Show yourself.'

Roisin froze. There was nothing for it. She mooched forth. 'Morning, Bronagh.'

'Jaysus wept, look at the state of you! You're the poster girl for the evils of alcohol at Christmastime so you are. Your eyes are like road maps. I could find my way all the way down to Kerry just looking in those.' She put down the papers she was holding in her hand.

'Not so loud, Bronagh. My head hurts.' Roisin tried squinting her eyes to see if that helped ease the throbbing. It didn't.

'Am I to take it, it was a good night then?'

Roisin nodded.

'Then why do you look like someone just stole the last piece of your pie?'

'I made an eejit of myself, that's why.'

'Really, I'd never believe that?'

Roisin wasn't sure whether Bronagh was taking the mickey or not. 'Well, I did.'

Bronagh studied her face and raised a sympathetic smile as she made a clucking sound. 'Ah, c'mon now, it can't be that bad. Tell your aunty Bronagh all about it.'

Roisin felt a little like she was standing in front of a schoolteacher as she bowed her head, her hands clasped in front of her while she confided in the receptionist how her evening had been going really well until she'd had a reality check as to her situation. 'He's only in his twenties, Bronagh. Sure, what would he want with me. Anyway,' she shrugged. 'I began knocking back the tequila sunrises and the rest is history.'

'That's not so bad. You won't be the only one to get a little too merry this time of year.'

'I tripped over leaving the restaurant and fell in a heap near the entrance.' Her face flamed because even in her inebriated state she'd felt the curious stares of the other diners on her. Shay had helped her up, checking she hadn't hurt herself, before taking a firm grip of her and hustling her out of the restaurant and into a taxi.

'Oh.'

'He was a gentleman, saw me all the way to the sofa upstairs. He fetched me a big glass of water and listened to me ramble on. I think I told him we weren't a good match due to him being footloose and fancy free and me having enough baggage to sink the Titanic, but that's not to say I didn't find him highly rideable. Ah Jaysus, Bronagh I can't believe I said that. Anyway I must have fallen asleep at some point, and that's when he made his escape because I woke up alone on the sofa with a terrible crick in my neck as the sun was coming up.' Roisin rubbed her temples. She was old enough to know better. *Never, ever again.*

Bronagh opened her drawer. 'Here,' she held out the packet of biscuits. 'I think you need one of these.'

Roisin took the custard cream and nibbled it, relishing the sweetness.

'Don't be too hard on yourself, Roisin. You've had an awful lot of changes this year and you were bound to let off steam some time. As for having luggage—'

'It's baggage, Bronagh.' Roisin managed a weak smile.

'Whatever, you know what I mean. There's not many of us who get through life without picking up a few heavy bags along the way. I don't know why you're making a fuss about being a few years older than your man, either.'

'Nearly ten years older, a whole decade, Bronagh.'

Bronagh flapped her hand. 'Age is just a number. Do you like him?'

'I do, he's a very nice man.'

'And he obviously likes you, suitcases and all so, there you go. I've seen that beautiful bouquet in the guests' lounge. Cut yourself some slack, Roisin. You're not after marrying him, you went out for dinner and a few drinks that's all.'

'Too many drinks, and I couldn't marry him because then I'd be a bigamist.'

'You're as bad as your sisters with an answer for everything.'

'Sorry, I know you're trying to help.' Roisin licked the crumbs off her bottom lip which felt dry and cracked from sleeping with her mouth open all night.

Bronagh was mollified. 'Roisin, I've been around the block a few times.'

She was fond of that saying, Roisin thought, finding it very hard to imagine Bronagh doing any such thing, but she'd obviously had a life outside of O'Mara's. It was just one they'd not been privy to.

'And if there's one thing I know it's this.' Bronagh's expression was sage. 'We women tend to spoil things for ourselves by spinning things round and round in our heads. Things we have no control over. We weave our own version of events. Save your energy, Rosi, I'd put money on him phoning to check how you're feeling today.'

'Do you think?' Roisin wasn't sure she wanted him to. The part of her that wanted to throw caution to the wind and be damned, desperately wanted to hear his voice. To know she hadn't blown things. The other part, the sensible mother part, thought it best if they just left things alone. She wasn't right for him, he wasn't right for her so why pursue it? She squinted again, her head hurt too much for all this analysis.

'I think. Now why don't you get yourself down those stairs and see what Mrs Flaherty can whip up to sort you out and next time I see you make sure you've brushed that hair of yours.

Is it a new look you were after with the you know?' She pointed at Roisin's fringe..

'No, it's a long story and one I definitely don't want to talk about.' Roisin leaned in and gave the receptionist a quick hug, 'Thanks, Bronagh.' Straightening up, she tried to smooth her fringe down with her hands.

Bronagh patted her hand. 'Go on. Away with you now.'

Before she headed off down the stairs, she poked her head around the door to the guests' lounge and there on the coffee table was the beautiful bunch of flowers Shay had presented her with last night. She recalled the boyishly shy look on his face as he handed them to her and her heart ached. Why did life have to be so hard sometimes?

'WHERE'S MY BOY?' MRS Flaherty demanded, releasing Roisin from a bearlike embrace and giving her the once over.

'He'll be in to see you later, Mrs Flaherty. He stayed at Mammy's last night,' Roisin explained.

'So as you could have a night out, by the looks of things.' The dumpling cheeked cook, whose apron straining around her middle bore the hallmarks of a busy morning at the stove, made a tutting sound.

Roisin mumbled, 'I wish I hadn't now.'

'Ah well, good sense is as important as good food and since you obviously had no sense last night it'll have to be the good food. A rasher sandwich do you?'

'Oh, yes please, Mrs Flaherty, nobody makes a rasher sandwich as good as yours and do you think there's a chance of a fried egg going in there too?' Roisin tried her luck and, watching Mrs Flaherty puff up proudly at the compliment, she knew her luck was in because there was nothing Mrs Flaherty liked more than her food being enjoyed.

'Sit yourself down and tell me what's been happening since I last saw you,' she said, wielding the fry pan with expertise as Roisin brought her up to date with how she and Noah were getting on in London. Roisin felt better already. She was at home in the kitchen with its delicious smells that always transported her back to her childhood. Mrs Flaherty's kitchen, as they all thought of it, had always been a place of sanctuary where something tasty usually got passed their way. By the time she'd brought the cook up to speed, the rashers were being placed between two thick slabs of buttered, real butter mind, soda bread. The finishing touch was an egg cooked on both sides. She plopped it on a plate and Roisin took it from her reverently.

'Thank you. Food of the Gods this is, Mrs Flaherty.'

Mrs Flaherty wiped her hands on her apron. 'You can earn your keep by helping clear the tables when you're finished.'

Roisin nodded, her mouth too full to speak. She ate in silence, greedily gobbling the sandwich down and already beginning to feel like there was a real possibility she may be able to rejoin the human race after all.

'That was wonderful, thank you.' She made herself a milky, sugary cup of tea, which she gulped at before stacking her dishes in the dishwasher, while Mrs Flaherty began to tackle the frying pan and other pots in the sudsy sink water. She hadn't forgotten her promise and she felt capable of nattering politely with the guests now she was fed and watered, so she ventured into the dining room. The tables were laid with white cloths and the walls of what once would have been servants' quarters were adorned with black and white prints of the Dublin of old. A handful of guests were still enjoying the remains of breakfast, mopping up the last of their yolk with a slice of bread or enjoying a leisurely cup of tea. She smiled and introduced herself before asking an older couple if they were enjoying their stay.

'We are thank you, dear,' the woman, who looked a little older than Mammy in her sensible cardigan and blouse, replied. She would not be the sort to come home from a holiday in Asia with her hair braided, Roisin decided, smiling back at her. Nor would she be likely to get about in trousers three sizes too small!

'We go home tomorrow, in time for Christmas.'

'And where would home be?'

'We're from Sligo,' the woman added, beaming proudly.

'Oh lovely.' Roisin had never been there. The only thing she knew about Sligo was Westlife came from there.

Her husband put his teacup down. 'The wife here, wanted to do her Christmas shopping in Dublin. We'll have to hire our own bus to get home with the amount of parcels she's been after buying. Spoils the grandchildren rotten. In my day it was an orange in the stocking if you were lucky.'

'Don't believe a word of it, he's worse than me when it comes to the grandchildren and it wasn't just an orange. I remember your dear old mam telling me you got a peashooter when you were ten and menaced the village with the thing.'

They smiled across the table at each other with the warmth of a life lived well together.

'My son's five and he's the only grandson and nephew so I expect his stocking will have more than an orange and peashooter in it too.' She smiled from one to the other. 'A Merry Christmas to you both and safe journey home.' Roisin moved on. The table at the far end of the room was ready to be cleared but as she made her way toward it, she spied a dapper gentleman who seemed lost in his thoughts as he sat with a plate of toast in front of him. He had sandy colouring, the sort that didn't show the grey hairs, and she guessed he would have had freckles in his youth. Either way this wouldn't do, Roisin thought. Mrs Flaherty would have conniptions if the toast were returned to the kitchen with her homemade marmalade jam untouched.

'A penny for them?'

The man blinked. He had bright, intelligent blue eyes, framed by neatly trimmed eyebrows. He looked surprised and mustn't have seen her approach the table, Roisin thought. It was then she spotted the book on the table. When We Were Brave, by Cliona Whelan, the book she'd had signed by the author just the other day for Aisling. She gestured toward the book and told the man she'd met Cliona Whelan, the author, at a signing. At the mention of her name his face seemed to transform as he looked at her keenly. 'You met Clio you say?' He was American with a clipped, cool accent.

Roisin nodded, her curiosity piqued. 'I did, well insomuch as she signed the copy of the book I bought for my sister as a Christmas present at Easons.' No need to tell him about the Christmas photo debacle.

'Have you read it?'

'No, although I read a review of it in the paper and it sounds very good.'

He nodded. "It is. It's brilliant but Clio always was brilliant.'

'Oh, you know her?'

'I do, yes, from a long time ago.'

'Is that why you've come to Dublin? To catch up with her again?'

'I'm hoping to, my dear. I've invited her to Christmas dinner at the Merrion but whether she'll come.' He shrugged. 'Well, a lot of water's gone under the bridge. I can only hope. My name's Gerald. Gerald Byrne, I'm from Boston but you can call me Gerry.'

'Roisin Quealey but I used to be Roisin O'Mara.' She explained her connection to the guesthouse and he invited her to sit down.

She did so and he placed a hand on the book. 'It's our story you know. Mine and Clio's. Only the ending is different. The story in this book has a happier ending than ours did. I'd like to make mine and Clio's ending different too.'

Roisin forgot all about everything as she sat transfixed by the story he told her.

Chapter 23

'It's lovely being ladies who lunch,' Mammy said, her arms linked firmly through Moira and Roisin's. All three of their faces were only visible in the gaps between the hats and scarves they'd donned as they stamped their feet against the cold, waiting for the lights to change so as to cross over to Baggot Street. An impromptu lunch had been Mammy's bright idea and they'd opted to walk to Quinn's bistro, aware of the amount of overeating they would be doing from hereon in until the New Year. Aisling, who'd had a successful morning shopping, had checked to make sure Quinn saved them a table.

She'd said to Roisin it would be a chance to get to know Cindy a little better. 'I've to be back at O'Mara's for three to meet the American group off the bus, they're back from their tour of the south and I want to make sure all their Christmas Day dinner reservations are confirmed,' she'd said shrugging into her coat before they left.

Baggot Street's foot traffic was busy, Roisin noticed, as the lights changed at last and they made their way across the road, merging in with the Christmas shoppers. Aisling and Cindy, their heads bent as they talked and tottered in impractical shoes, were slightly ahead of them. Cindy, not used to the cold, looked like a well-endowed Russian Cossack with her faux fur hat, Roisin thought, smirking as a middle-aged man who should know better had an incident with a lamppost.

Served him right for being so fixated on the blonde apparition mincing down Baggot.

'It was good of your brother to offer to take Noah to the cinema,' Maureen said. 'It will be nice for the two men of the family to get to know one another better.'

'It was,' Roisin agreed. Patrick had surprised her with how much attention he'd given Noah and she'd been pleased when he suggested he and Noah go and see the Disney Christmas flick showing at the IMAX. Noah had been jumping up and down at the prospect of a boys' outing. 'I hope Pat doesn't let him have the extra-large popcorn. If I know Noah, he'll plump for it but he'll make himself sick, stuffing all that down on top of the rasher sandwich Mrs Flaherty made him.' Mind you, she wasn't in a position to talk the way she'd snaffled hers down and now here she was off for a slap-up lunch! Thank goodness for yoga pants.

'They'll be grand. Don't worry so, Roisin,' Maureen said. 'So, are you going to tell us how your evening went with your man? I hope you changed the sheets in your room.'

'Mammy, nothing happened!'

'I should hope not on a first date!' Maureen was indignant. 'You girls' minds dwell in the gutter so they do. What I meant was your room smelt like a brewery when I poked my head around the door and as it's a full house tonight, I'd hope you'd have at least put clean linen on the bed. I'm looking forward to us all being together under one roof again. And it's been far too long since the O'Mara family attended Midnight Mass together.'

'So, there was no riding,' Moira lamented, looking disappointed.

'No.'

'Moira O'Mara!'

'Did you kiss?' Moira ignored her mammy.

'Moira, mind your own business.' Roisin peered around their mammy and eyeballed her sister.

'Ah, Rosi, that's not fair, especially after all the hard work I did sorting you and your fringe out,' Moira moaned.

'Will you be seeing him again do you think?' Maureen asked.

'I don't know,' Rosi said. Her head was beginning to hurt again.

'Jaysus, it's harder getting information out of you than a cold war spy,' Moira muttered.

'She always did play her cards close to her chest,' Maureen added, nearly tripping as Moira pulled them to a stop in order to admire the vibrant new Revlon display in the window of Boots.

'That's your woman who looks like a man one, isn't it? I danced to that at the yacht club dinner.'

'Shania Twain, Man I feel Like a Woman. Read the slogan, Mammy!' Moira rolled her eyes. 'I like that shade of purple.'

'It's lavender,' Maureen said.

'It's not lavender, that sounds old ladyish,' Moira bounced back.

'She looks well on it, your Shania one, doesn't she?' Maureen said wistfully.

'She does,' Roisin agreed, though she was unsure why they were all stood staring at her poster. It was tempting fate in her opinion because she wouldn't put it past Mammy to break into a line dancing routine. She kept a firm grip of her arm just in case.

'Do you think she uses the magic skin plumpy thing-a-me-bobs that are all the go at the moment?' Maureen asked.

'Serum do you mean, Mammy?' Roisin said.

Maureen nodded, 'Yes, semen.'

'SERUM! And yes, for sure.' Moira nodded knowledgably as though she was privy to Shania's night time beauty routine.

'Do you think I could do with a bit of plumping?'

Both sisters peered at their mammy's face.

'Your face has plenty of plump, so it does,' Moira said.

Roisin recalled her exchange with Aisling where her sister had told her their mammy had been acting a little strangely since the yacht club dinner. 'Why do you need plumping all of a sudden?' Her eyes narrowed as she studied her mammy's face.

'A woman of certain years is bound to wonder from time to time whether she might need plumping.' Maureen looked shifty.

'Well you don't. You're fine the way you are,' Roisin snapped, pulling her and Moira away from the window. 'Come on, Cindy and Ash will be on dessert by the time we get there.'

THE FAMILIAR AND QUINTESSENTIAL, whitewashed building, with its brass nameplate, that was Quinn's, came into their line of sight and Roisin found herself anticipating the cosy and warm atmosphere she knew they'd find inside. They bustled in through the door in time to witness Alasdair fawning all over Cindy.

'I never thought I'd see you again, my darling!'

Cindy looked bewildered, 'I'm sorry but I don't think we've met before. This is my first time visiting Dublin.'

'Ah non!' The flamboyant maître de clapped a hand to his chest. 'You must remember! It is me, the Fellini to your Ekberg. La Dolce Vita, my darling.' He blew her a kiss and Cindy looked at Aisling slightly alarmed by his carry-on. Aisling didn't appear fazed; in fact she was smiling.

She leaned in towards her getting a strong whiff of her sugary sweet perfume and stage whispered, 'Alasdair has had more past lives than I've had hot dinners. He's famous for them. He even gets a mention in the Lonely Planet. He's what you'd call a Dublin icon and he's very good for business. My guess is he's decided you were Anita Ekberg when he was Frederico Fellini.' Aisling, copping an eyeful of cleavage as Cindy undid the buttons on her coat, could see where he'd gotten the idea from.

Cindy's mouth formed an 'O' as though she got it. She didn't; they were all a bit mad in Ireland from what she'd seen, but she let Alasdair help her out of her coat, nonetheless.

Maureen pushed forward, more than happy to be on the receiving end of one of Alasdair's effusive greetings. He didn't disappoint her, exclaiming over how divine she was looking – how divine they were all looking as he took their coats and whisked away the pile of hats and scarves so they disappeared like magic. Paula, the waitress working the lunchtime Christmas Eve shift, saw them to their table which was in a prime spot in the middle of the heaving restaurant. They sat themselves down and Roisin looked on enviously as Cindy fluffed her hair and it formed a becoming halo around her face despite her Cossack hat. She fluffed her own hair knowing it would have moulded itself into the shape of the woollen hat she'd pulled down low enough to keep her ears warm on the walk over.

Aisling looked pleased as Cindy oohed and aahed over how "Irish" the restaurant was. The chatter filling the inviting space around them was convivial and interspersed with the sounds of glasses clinking, the chink of knives and forks on plates, and bursts of laughter. The aroma of hearty food, the sort that would stick to your ribs, clung to the air, and Roisin's tummy grumbled despite her hearty breakfast.

'I love the wooden beams and the fire, it's so cute,' Cindy gushed, and Aisling puffed up proudly although she deflated slightly when Cindy followed this up with a giggling, 'It reminds me of the cottage out of Snow White and the Seven Dwarfs or Goldilocks.' Aisling excused herself eager to find Quinn so she could introduce him to her brother's new girlfriend, hoping she'd keep her fairy-tale comparisons to herself.

'Will we have wine?' Maureen asked, looking from one to the other and shaking her head as her eyes settled on Moira. 'Well not for you, Moira, obviously.' She turned to Roisin. 'And given your mushy peas complexion I think you'd do better on the Coca-Cola like your sister.' She smiled at Cindy, 'There's no reason Aisling, Cindy and myself shouldn't enjoy a tipple though.'

'I'll stick with the mineral water, thanks, Maureen,' Cindy dimpled. 'I have to keep an eye on my calorie intake.'

Maureen looked down at her own middle.

Aisling returned with Quinn, who was looking handsome and incredibly immaculate in his chef's whites. It always amazed Roisin, given his profession, how he kept them so clean. If it were her let loose in the kitchen, she'd have more sauce down her front than simmering in the pots! 'How're you all,' he grinned. 'It's an honour having all the beautiful O'Mara women here together. And, Cindy, it's grand to have you here all the way from Los Angeles. Welcome.'

'Get away with you,' Maureen said, preening. She loved being made a fuss of. It had been a highlight in her social calendar year when she'd treated Rosemary Farrell from her rambling group to a birthday lunch at Quinn's. He'd made them feel like proper VIP guests and Rosemary had been very impressed, especially when the chef gave them his personal lunch recommendations. 'Now then what would you recommend we order today, Quinn?' she asked as Paula passed around the menus.

'Well now, Maureen, I know you're partial to coddle and it's particularly tasty today. The sausages are specialty free range pork and I used new potatoes.'

'What's coddle?' Cindy simpered over the top of her menu. Aisling frowned. Was she flirting with Quinn? She was one of those women who flirted not even knowing she was flirting.

She looked at Quinn who was oblivious to her charms as he replied theatrically, 'Only the finest meal in Ireland.'

'It's sausage and potato boiled up in one pot,' Moira stated.

'Oh, sounds, um, wonderful.'

'That's settled then,' Mammy said. 'Cindy and I will have the coddle. Aisling will you share a carafe of the house red with me?'

Aisling nodded, yes, she would, and Quinn kissed her on the cheek. It wasn't all he did.

'I saw that pat on the bottom,' Maureen tutted, and he gave her a grin that made him look like a naughty schoolboy, before leaving Paula to take care of them.

She scribbled down their orders. Two coddles and three Dublin Bay prawns. 'Easy,' she said with a smile before taking their order through to the kitchen.

Maureen rummaged in her bag which was hanging on the side of her chair and retrieved a pen and notepad. 'There's no such thing as a free lunch, ladies,' she announced looking very businesslike. 'To save squabbling in the kitchen over who's doing what tomorrow I thought we'd write a list allocating all the jobs to be done.'

Moira interrupted, 'Bags not stuff the turkey. I can't stand sticking my hand up its arse.'

'Moira!'

'I'll do the turkey, Mammy, and once I've got it in the oven, I'll set the table, oh and don't forget Quinn's made the plum pudding. It's curing as we speak.' Aisling smiled, knowing if she put her hand up for this then she wouldn't get the job of scrubbing potatoes or prepping the Brussels.

Maureen scribbled earnestly before looking at Cindy. 'Now then, Cindy, how about we put you on carrots, parsnips and the Brussels. Hmm, and,' she chewed the end of the pen for a moment, 'Moira you're on potatoes and you can help your sister decorate the dining room. Roisin, you can be in charge of the smoked salmon starters and mulled wine.'

'What are you doing, Mammy?'

'I'm on the roast ham and bread sauce.'

'I don't suppose there's any point asking what Pat's going to be doing,' Aisling said.

'Sitting on his arse, that's what,' Moira said.

'Leave your brother alone, girls. Sure, he works hard all year, he deserves to put his feet up.'

All three sisters looked from one to another in mutual outrage. 'It's nearly the Millennium, Mammy, that kind of thinking went out with the dark ages,' Aisling said, but Mammy pretended she couldn't hear her as she stowed her pen and pad back in her bag. She decided to let it go, knowing she'd be wasting her breath and turned her attention to Moira and Cindy who were chatting.

Roisin glanced around the restaurant. There were no empty tables, she saw, as her eyes settled on the empty stage upon which two littlies were playing a game of chase. She pictured Shay standing there and remembered how their eyes had literally met over a crowded bar. Mammy talking in her ear brought her back to the here and now and her chat with their American guest, Gerry sprang to mind. 'Mammy,' she said her voice lowered so Aisling wouldn't overhear and have her Christmas surprise ruined, 'have you heard of Cliona Whelan?'

'Sure, of course I have, she's a fine journalist, and she was a role model in my day, so she was, for women in the workforce. She's written a book hasn't she?'

'She has, and, Mammy, you won't believe it, listen to this...' Roisin filled her in on the story Gerry, the guest she'd encountered over breakfast, had told her about his and Cliona's ill-fated romance back in the late nineteen-fifties. 'He told me she changed the names and the story's been fictionalised but at the core it's their story only in Cliona's book, instead of her staying in Dublin she goes to Boston and marries him. He claws his way up to the top echelon of American politics and she manages, against the odds, to carve a career for herself as a journalist. He said Cliona was always a woman before her time.'

'That's a big word, Roisin.'

'Echelon? I know, Gerry used it.'

'Well, it's quite the story. I'll have to read the book now and would you credit it, him staying at O'Mara's?'

'Yes, I couldn't believe it, especially with me having bought the book the day before for Aisling. She broke his heart he said. Although he came to understand her reasons for doing so.'

'And did he marry?'

'Eventually. He told me he followed the path laid out for him and when his parents steered him toward a woman from what they called "good stock" he went along with it. He married her but it didn't last. They had two children, boys who are grown up with children of their own now.'

'Did she, Cliona, I mean ever marry?'

'No, her work always came first. I read in the foreword of the book that she said it had to in the times she moved in, if she wanted to succeed.'

'She smashed through the glass ceiling alright, and it wouldn't have been easy.'

'It came at a cost, too. Do you think she'll meet him at the Merrion, Mammy?' Roisin had seen the look in Gerry's eyes when he spoke about Cliona and knew his heart would be broken if they didn't get a second chance at love.

'You're a softy you are.' Maureen patted her daughter's hand and looked pensive. 'I like to think we all deserve a second chance when it comes to love, Rosi, because life's too short to spend it sad.'

Again, there was something unsettling about the expression that passed over her mammy's face and Roisin squirmed in her seat, grateful when Paula appeared at the table and set about distributing the drinks. She was glad when the glass of red wine that was put in front of Mammy broke the strange spell that had settled over her.

Chapter 24

Roisin watched Cindy out of the corner of her eye. She had a ritualistic style of eating that was fascinating to observe. Her brother's girlfriend forked up another piece of sausage and held it to her pert little nose, which quivered delightedly as she sniffed at it. In that instance she reminded Roisin of Mr Nibbles. A look of bliss settled over her face just like it did the gerbil's when he had hold of a lettuce leaf but instead of nibbling at it gleefully like Noah's new pet did, she put the sausage back on her plate. She then cut a tiny sliver off and popped that in her mouth, pushing what remained of it to the side of her plate to keep company with the new potatoes that had been relegated there. Roisin counted twenty chews before she swallowed. She knew all about mindfulness, and it was something she tried to practise. Mindful eating, however, was something she, Mammy, and her sisters, who were like pigs at a trough when they were hungry, could do with a lot more practise at. She added it to her mental new year's resolution list. Cindy however was taking things to the extreme.

Roisin couldn't contain herself, she had to ask, 'Erm, Cindy, if you don't mind me asking, why are you sniffing your food?'

Cindy flashed her a blinding smile. 'Of course, I don't mind. The Ciccone-Scent diet is the latest craze sweeping through Hollywood. All the A-listers are trying it and getting great results.'

'Oh, is it a sniff your food but don't eat it diet then?' Roisin could quite see you'd get results doing that.

Cindy laughed, it sounded high pitched and girly. 'It's not quite that simple, Roisin.' She stabbed in the direction of the new potatoes with her fork. 'I don't touch potatoes in any form because they're full of carbs. Carbs are the enemy. But us girls already knew that, right?'

Roisin nodded, looking everywhere but at her own plate where she'd already wolfed down the French fries that had been served with her prawns. As for Moira, she seemed to be trying to see how many of the deep-fried potato sticks she could get in her mouth at once. Mammy's, like Roisin's, were long gone. They'd both saved the prawns for last.

'Okay, so as a devotee of the Ciccone-Scent diet, I avoid all carbs and only eat half of the protein served on my plate. Dr Ciccone's research shows that inhaling your food before you eat it tricks your stomach into thinking it's full and that way you only need to eat half your normal meal size. Makes sense, right?'

Um, no, it sounded mad, Roisin thought, as she nodded that yes it did.

'I love it because it's so easy to follow and I don't have to buy any fancy food. It really works too. I, dropped five pounds before Patrick and I flew out of LA.' Her eyes drifted down to Roisin's midriff and she automatically sucked her stomach in.

'You must be very disciplined, Cindy. Sure, I couldn't be doing with sniffing and not eating.'

'Oh, you could if you lived in LA, Roisin. Everybody does it.'

Roisin was very glad she lived in London.

Cindy pushed her plate away while the rest of them carried on shovelling in their food. Roisin was feeling panicked by the idea of only being allowed to inhale her food and so she was getting her prawns from plate to mouth in record time. 'Excuse me, I'm just off to powder my nose.' Cindy got up and caused several male patrons to begin choking on their fare as she sashayed past.

Mammy elbowed Moira, pointing, 'Sure, look at your man there. He's as bad as your Hugh Hefner Playboy one.'

Mammy and Moira launched into a discussion on everything that was wrong with a man, who was clearly old enough to be Cindy's grandfather, having impure thoughts about a young woman.

'He wants to tie a knot in it at his age,' Moira said.

Once Cindy was out of earshot, Aisling leaned in close to Roisin, gesturing in Cindy's direction. 'Do you know what she's after telling me and Moira?'

'That she sniffs her food?'

'What?'

'Never mind.' Roisin couldn't be bothered explaining the whole Ciccone-Scent diet thing.

Aisling shook her head. 'You're an eejit. She told us Patrick was desperate to come home to Ireland for Christmas.'

'Really?' Roisin had always got the feeling Patrick was rather lukewarm when it came to Dublin. It wasn't fast enough or glitzy enough for him. Oh, she knew right enough he loved them all. As much as Patrick loved anyone who wasn't himself. It was just, Patrick.

He'd never been any different. Roisin could remember Mammy having to drag him away from shop windows when he'd caught sight of his reflection as a young lad. 'People will think it's the underwear on the mannequin you're after drooling over Patrick,' she'd said tugging at his arm. When they'd reached their teens, the battle of the bathroom had begun in earnest and Daddy had taken to timing them; turned out Patrick spent the longest getting ready of a morning. In the end they'd been allocated five-minute time slots apiece. Patrick had been most put out, but then it was the eighties and hair was big.

'I know, I was surprised too, but she said he's been missing us all something terrible and that he told her Christmas is a time for family.'

'Stop it.' Roisin wasn't sure this was her brother they were talking about.

'I'm only repeating what Cindy told me.'

Roisin felt a surge of love for her brother. Beneath all that shiny polish he was still the Pat she'd grown up with.

'Apparently he's ashamed of the way he behaved after Dad died. But you know Pat, he never could say he was sorry.'

That was true. Many a time Mammy had marched him in front of his sisters and ordered him to apologise for some misdemeanour or other like giving Barbie a crew cut so as he could enlist her in his army or standing on their dolls house, which had been demolished in a surprise attack by his army. The word had seemed to get stuck in his throat as he was held firm by Mammy. In the end he'd mutter something that came out in a big whoosh and Mammy would release him having decided to interpret it as an apology.

'Cindy says he feels bad about pushing so hard for Mammy to sell O'Mara's after Daddy died. He doesn't know what got into him.'

'So, he should,' Roisin said.

Aisling nodded. It had been her who'd been the most affected by his behaviour. She was the one who'd fitted her life in around the guesthouse to ensure it stayed in the family.

'Did she say why he was so keen to offload it? Was it to back some venture over in the States?' That was what they'd all thought, after all.

'No, apparently not. Well not entirely anyway. He thinks it was a kneejerk reaction to Daddy dying. A bit like Mammy, you know, with her wanting a fresh start over in Howth. He wanted shot of it because the memories were too painful. Everywhere he looked he saw Daddy and he didn't know how to express how he was feeling.'

'So, he came across as an arrogant, bullying, money grabbing arse instead, who dragged his sulky self back to Los Angeles.'

'Pretty much, but guess what?'

'What?'

'He's been going to therapy.'

'No!'

'Yes.'

'He's a proper American now, so he is.' Roisin tried to imagine her brother sitting on a white sofa talking about his emotions, but couldn't.

'I know. I think Cindy's good for him. She obviously brings out his softer side because he finally seems to have realised there's more to life than making money and driving flash cars.'

A leopard didn't change its spots did it? Therapy or no therapy, Roisin thought. Patrick would always have a hankering for the finer things in life and chasing after the almighty dollar.

Appearances mattered a lot to her brother. She glanced at Cindy making her way back from the Ladies and rested her case. He'd never go for a wallflower type simply because she was a nice person. Still Daddy's death had obviously hit him hard, just as it had all of them. Roisin sighed into her glass of cola. Grief and the way they'd reacted to it hadn't been straightforward. They'd all acted out in different ways, his passing leaving a gaping hole in all their lives. Patrick had been the only one seemingly untouched, blustering in and pushing for O'Mara's to be sold, although apparently it had been just that, bluster. A cover for the rawness he felt from Daddy's passing.

'Anyway, I've decided Christmas is a time for forgiveness so I'm going to give Pat a second chance.' Aisling stated, and Roisin noticed her cheeks were flushed the colour of the wine.

'Good for you, Ash. We all deserve second chances.' She said as her sister announced she was going to have to forfeit dessert and make tracks back to the guesthouse. Second chances was a theme that kept popping up and her mind drifted back to Shay. She looked up and blinked, not sure whether she was hallucinating or not because there like a mirage, walking toward their table, was Shay.

Chapter 25

'I called in to see you at O'Mara's. I wanted to catch up with you before I head to Castlebeg later this afternoon. See how you were feeling. Bronagh told me you were here for lunch and it's only around the corner,' he shrugged. 'So here I am. I hope you don't mind me gatecrashing like this?' He grinned apologetically at Roisin and then at the others. She blinked again several times, still not convinced she hadn't dreamed this moment into reality. She flinched as a foot connected with her ankle, Aisling's way of reassuring her she was very much in the here and now. She was reminded too that she owed this man an apology for her behaviour the previous night. The memory of her waffling on made her squirm but before she could speak Mammy leapt in.

'Oh no, she doesn't mind at all, do you, Roisin? I'm Roisin's mammy, Maureen, by the way, seeing as my daughter's forgotten her manners. We've not had the pleasure. How do you do?' Mammy beamed holding a hand out. Shay took her outstretched hand and for the briefest of seconds, Roisin thought he was going to kiss it but he didn't. He shook it, smiling at her mam in a way that made her blush. Mind, it didn't take much to make Mammy blush once she was on her second glass of the red.

'I can see where Roisin gets her good looks from.'

Maureen looked like one of those specialty Japanese fish you take your life in your hands by eating at this, and Roisin couldn't help but smile. It was cheesy but coming from Shay it didn't *seem* clichéd. It came across as genuine. She'd have words with Moira later too, she decided seeing her sister going red from the effort not to laugh at Mammy's puffer fish impersonation. They were so embarrassing the lot of them. Even Aisling and Cindy were looking eagerly at Shay as though he were going to bestow them each with a compliment like some sort of fairy godmother who'd rocked up in battle-worn denim. She couldn't blame them, she supposed, because he did look gorgeous. Not in the clean-cut coiffed way of her brother but in a rugged, earthy way, that made her think things that would definitely make Mammy tell her to get her mind out of the gutter. She couldn't understand why she kept picturing him with a Stetson on his head, though. She'd no idea she had a thing for cowboys until she met him. Cindy, clearing her throat daintily, galvanised her and she introduced the blonde bombshell to him.

As she held onto his hand longer than necessary, Roisin gave him a mental ten out of ten for keeping his eyes trained on her face the whole time. No mean feat given the heaving bosom just under his nose. She bit her bottom lip as Aisling elbowed her and whispered, 'She'll start singing Happy Birthday Mr President in a minute.'

'Bunch up, girls,' Mammy ordered, giving Cindy a look that made her drop Shay's hand like a hot potato. She scanned the room for a spare chair but Shay stopped her.

'Actually, Maureen, I wondered if I might be able to borrow Roisin for a few minutes.'

The puffer fish was back and was just about jumping up and down on her seat with the excitement of it all.

Roisin got up from her chair, feeling the hot stares of her family on her back as they excused themselves, and she followed his lead past the toilets and out the backdoor. *What had he come to say?* The door led outside to the car park which, although full of cars, didn't have a soul in sight. There was a pot on the ground near the backdoor full of cigarette butts. Hardy lot, smokers she thought, standing outside for their fix in all weather conditions. She could smell that faint greasy odour of stale fat from the extractor fan whirring overhead.

'Sorry to drag you out in the cold.'

'Not at all.' Her breath was misty in the chill air. She leaned against the cold brick wall shoving her hands deep into the pockets of her jeans for warmth. She owed him an apology and she decided she better jump in first and get it over with. 'Listen, Shay, I'm sorry about getting myself in such a state last night and the way I went on. I don't know what you must have thought of me but it's been ages since I've had a night out and I got carried away. Can you please just forget everything I said?'

His eyes twinkled, 'What, even the bit about me being highly rideable?'

'Ah Jaysus.' She freed her hands to cover her face, peeking through her fingers at him. 'Don't remind me.'

'I'm teasing.' He pulled her hands away from her face and kept hold of them. They were swallowed up by his and she marvelled that hands that size could be so quick and nimble with the fiddle. She wondered what else those hands might be good at. 'You don't need to apologise, Rosi. I had a great craic, the best I've had in ages, and you were hilarious by the way.'

'I was?' She swallowed hard. She couldn't recall having said anything particularly witty.

'Yeah, when you launched into *Who Let the Dogs Out* on the way home, I just about lost it. I loved the little paws you made with your hands and the woofing was class.'

'Please tell me I didn't?'

'Oh, you did alright.' His smile and the way it worked the dimple in his left cheek made her forget she was cold and embarrassed.

'Anyway, there's a reason I dragged you out here.'

'Oh yes?' Roisin hadn't a clue what he wanted but looking at him right then and there she'd happily throw all that nonsense about her being too old for him and their lives being too different or the timing being all wrong out the window. Life was messy, it didn't run to a timetable.

'Yeah, I wanted to tell you something before I go away.'

Roisin couldn't tear her eyes away from him and her body began to react very strangely to the proximity of his. A heat was coursing from her stomach to her chest and her limbs were tingling. How was it possible for anyone to smell as good as he did? It was a musky, spiced scent that made her nose want to twitch like Cindy's had over her sausage. She was aware of his thumbs gently stroking the back of her hands and more than anything she wanted to stand on her tippy toes so she could kiss him. It was a seize the day moment but then she remembered, *I had prawns, PRAWNS for lunch. Oh my God, what was I thinking?* Now was not the time to retrieve the tube of mints from her handbag. She couldn't surreptitiously pop one out and say, 'I'm getting ready just in case you decide to kiss me.'

'I think you're a very special lady, Roisin, and I want you to give me a chance. I promise I won't push you too fast and I'll respect what you say because I understand there's Noah to think about but please, can you give us a go?' There was a sudden vulnerability about him as a lock of his hair fell into his eyes and he looked at her almost shyly waiting for her reaction.

'Oh,' was all she could come up with. She hadn't expected that but there was no time to mull over what he'd said or to worry about Dublin Bay crustaceans or the fact her fringe was sitting two-thirds of the way up her forehead because he was leaning in towards her. Their noses bumped and she was about to giggle nervously, not quite believing what was about to happen, but it was silenced by his lips finding hers. They brushed one another's softly and then they broke apart looking into each other's eyes with surprise. Shay brushed a stray curl from her cheek.

'You have no idea how badly I have wanted to do that from the very first moment I saw you.'

'Really?'

'Really.' His mouth sought hers again and she parted her lips slightly to receive him. His fingers entwined through hers and she was glad when he pulled her close holding her steady because she was in danger of sliding down the wall if he let her go. As the heat of his mouth on hers intensified, Roisin wasn't aware of anything other than the feel of his body pressing into hers and the sweet taste of him. It was as though the world around them had ceased to exist. Nothing mattered but losing herself in this moment because, like Mammy had said, everybody deserved a second chance at love and maybe this was hers.

Chapter 26

M oira, in her role as the youngest girl in the family, lit the
candle and placed it well away from the curtains on the
windowsill in the living room facing the street below. The
Green across the road was in darkness, the bare branches of the
trees' ghostly spectres, but the road was busy with cars streaming home from Midnight Mass.

'Watch your hair, Moira. Jesus, Mary and Joseph we don't
need that on Christmas Eve,' Mammy called from the kitchen,
where she was cutting everybody a generous chunk of seed
cake. 'Nobody's going to bed without a hot chocolate and a
slice of my cake. It's traditional, isn't that right Quinn?' she ordered, as they all found somewhere to flop, weary from the
long, but enjoyable evening. Quinn nodded as he stirred the
pot in which he was brewing the bedtime drink. The restaurant
had closed early and he'd joined them for Midnight Mass. He
and Aisling were taking over Room 5 which was empty for
the night. Moira and Mammy were topping and tailing and
Patrick and Cindy were back in his old room. Roisin and Noah
were in Aisling's room. It was a case of musical beds but they'd
all worked in together, apart from Moira who was muttering
about Mammy being a bed hog. Tom was spending Christmas
Eve with his family as his sister was home from America but he
planned on joining them later in the day tomorrow.

'I hope you weren't mean with the caraway seeds like last
year, Mammy,' Moira called back.

'There's more seeds than cake, I'll have you know.' Maureen was indignant. 'And they were a ridiculous price last year, so they were.'

'Why's Aunty Moira lighting a candle?' Noah asked from where he was cuddled on his mam's knee. He was playing with a lock of her hair, twisting it around his finger the way he always did when he was tired.

'It's to provide a welcome light for Mary and Joseph,' Roisin explained, enjoying the feel of his warm weight on her lap. He was dead on his feet, poor love. It had been a big day and the evening had been just as big if not bigger.

Her mind drifted back to that afternoon. She'd arranged to meet Shay the day after St Stephens Day and she could hardly wait. His kiss had gone down as her best ever Christmas present. She'd floated home from Quinn's, ignoring Cindy's smirking gaze and the one hundred and one questions from Moira and Mammy about what she'd gotten up to in the car park and why her lipstick was smudged halfway across her face. She'd been telling them to mind their own business as they barrelled in through the door of O'Mara's to find Aisling in full hostess mode. She'd been milling about chatting to the American tour party who'd not long arrived back at the guesthouse while Bronagh busied herself checking them all in.

Maureen had instantly slotted into her old role, and Roisin and Moira grabbed Cindy to make their escape. By the time they'd reached the bottom of the stairs she'd launched into a conversation about Irish Christmas traditions with a couple from Maine. Pooh's effusive greeting when she'd opened the door had brought Roisin back down to earth, not to mention flying backwards and Moira and Cindy had done a wary sidestep all the way through to the lounge. They'd found Patrick and Noah sitting on the floor surrounded by coloured paper.

Patrick had explained they'd collected Pooh and Mr Nibbles after their film so as Mammy wouldn't have to drive back to Howth later that afternoon. 'That one who does the cleaning is a bit strange isn't she?' he'd added.

'Idle Ita? In what way?' Roisin had asked.

'Well every time I head down the stairs, she pops out from one of the rooms like a fecking Jack in the Box and just stands there staring at me. It's unnerving, she reminds me of your one out of that Stephen King film.'

'Carrie.' That had come from Moira.

'Yeah, that's the one.'

'I think she's sweet on you, Pat.' Roisin recalled the housekeeper's excitement at the news Patrick was home.

'You can't blame her, honey. You are one gorgeous hunk of a man.' Cindy had draped herself over him while Moira made gagging noises.

'Look, Mummy,' Noah who'd been fed up with the lack of attention had cried. He'd held up the beginnings of a paper chain. 'Uncle Pat's teaching me how to make these.'

'Can we help,' she'd asked, and the three of them had sat down cross-legged next to the two boys to begin stapling and folding in earnest, while Pooh watched with his head resting on his paws and Mr Nibbles scrabbled sporadically in his cage. It had made Roisin nostalgic for her childhood, and Mammy, when she'd run out of delights to share with the tour group, had been delighted all over again with their efforts, declaring that the colourful chains would be used to decorate the dining room.

Indeed, the paper chains had looked festive once they'd draped them around the room, digging out the box of tinsel kept in the hall cupboard to add a bit of sparkle. The dining room had looked even more festive with a mug of the mulled wine, Aisling had made, warming their insides, and they'd been pleased with their efforts as they trooped back upstairs to watch the Late Late Toy Show Moira had recorded earlier that month for them all to watch. It had whiled away the hours until Midnight Mass.

Roisin cuddled Noah closer, rocking him as she used to when he was a baby. Her heart was full. He'd nodded off on her shoulder during the mass despite the hard wooden pew on which they were all perched. It had been a lovely evening she thought as she rested her face against his soft downy head. She inhaled the faint smell of frankincense which clung to his hair from the incense that had burned inside the church. Father Fitzpatrick's service had been brief, but to the point as befitted the time of night. Roisin had always enjoyed the carol singing at Midnight Mass, it was her favourite part because that was when it felt like Christmas to her. Not even Mammy bellowing Silent Night in her ear like a cow on heat could change that.

As for Mammy, well she'd been in seventh heaven surrounded by her whole family. It was a rare event these days and even rarer to get them all under God's roof. She'd told them all, in no uncertain terms, to be on their best behaviour just as she used to when they were small only this time, thanks be to God, she didn't spit on a hanky and start wiping at their faces. She'd had to have a quiet word with Patrick before they left when Cindy bounced into the living room announcing she was good to go. She'd told him if his girlfriend were to wave those things about, she currently had on display, during the Midnight Mass, Father Patrick might do himself an injury when he was swinging the incense and could he please suggest a more sedate choice of top. Patrick had huffed off, taking Cindy by the elbow and they'd returned a few minutes later with her clad in a snug white sweater and equally snug white pants. She looked like a Christmas angel Noah had told her, starstruck. A Christmas angel for Victoria's Secret perhaps, Roisin had thought, but she'd kept it to herself. Either way it had been enough of an improvement to satisfy Maureen and for her to introduce her to friends old and new as they'd gathered inside St Teresa's for the service.

There'd been a bit of a skirmish before things got underway when the O'Reilly sisters, both spinsters for obvious reasons, tried to squeeze in alongside Patrick. There'd only been enough room for one and the older of the two sisters, Elsie, had fallen into the aisle. She'd been helped up by Mr Kelly, recently widowed, and had been appeased when he patted the seat to suggest she squish in alongside him.

Sitting in the living room now, waiting for Mammy to dole out the cake as the old grandfather clock ticked that time was marching on, Roisin could hear the odd car horn as people full of the festive spirit made their way home from the church service. The church bells that had rung out through the city earlier were silent now and she guessed all across the country children would be fighting to stay awake in order to hear Santa's reindeer on the roof. The family had walked the short distance home from St Teresa's, their breath hanging like crystals in the air. They'd filed out of the church to calls of Merry Christmas to be greeted by a magical scene. The city had been dusted in an icing sugar snow sprinkle during the service. It had seen Mammy exclaim, 'The geese are being plucked in heaven tonight, so they are.'

'Here we are, one for you and one for you. No, Pooh, back to bed, chocolate and cake isn't good for you.' Roisin didn't like to say that it wasn't good for them either. Mammy began passing out the cake and true to her word it was loaded with the pungent anise flavoured seeds. Roisin settled Noah, whose eyes, despite his valiant efforts at staying awake long enough for hot chocolate and cake, were drooping next to her. She'd get Pat to carry him to bed because he'd be sound asleep in a minute or two. Taking the mug Quinn offered her and cupping it with both hands, the serviette on her lap with her half-eaten seed cake, she looked at her brothers and sisters and smiled. It was going to be a lovely, Christmas here at home all together, so it was.

Chapter 27

Roisin woke up to feel a warm hand tapping her on the side of her face. Her eyes fluttered reluctantly open just enough to see, unsurprisingly, that Noah was the culprit. Through her sleepy fog it dawned on her it was Christmas morning and she forced her eyes open properly, blinking several times. The ability of children to be wide awake the moment they opened their eyes amazed her once more as he began performing trampoline style bounces on the bed.

'Noah, you'll break the bed.'

'I'm making sure you're awake.'

'I'm awake. Merry Christmas, sweetheart.'

'Yay for Christmas!' He fist-bumped the air and Roisin smiled at his enthusiasm before cocking an ear. The house was silent. She glanced over at the bedside clock, it was eight am. It was nothing short of a miracle that Noah had slept this late and she tossed the covers aside as she remembered last year's obscene five thirty start. It was definitely time to get up, there was a lot to be done between now and four o'clock when their guests arrived for Christmas dinner. She knotted her dressing gown and followed her son's lead to the living room, where the first thing he did was race into the kitchen to check Santa had drunk the bottle of Guinness they'd left out for him. 'It's gone, Mum.'

'Thirsty work delivering all those presents.' She was guessing Patrick would have slept soundly after knocking that back.

At the word presents, Noah raced over to the tree to check his stocking. 'Mum, it's very heavy!' She flicked the kettle on and looked over in time to see him dragging it to the middle of the living room floor. Pooh bounced over to see what he was up to and, remembering his little friend, Noah dropped the stocking, ran to the fridge and retrieved a lettuce leaf which he gave to Mr Nibbles. 'You're doing a good job looking after him, Noah,' Roisin said, heaping a teaspoon of coffee into a mug and dropping the spoon with a clatter as she felt a snuffling where nobody should be snuffling at this time of the morning. 'Get away with you.' The dog looked thoroughly dejected and she spied the empty bowl on the newspaper near the pantry. 'Ah well, it is Christmas morning I suppose.' Holding her nose she lopped him off a slice of the meaty roll in the fridge and gave him a scoop of the dried food sitting on the corner of the bench. *There that should keep him otherwise occupied for the time being.* She made a pot of tea too, deciding it was time everyone was up because she couldn't possibly be expected to contain Noah from ripping into his stocking while they waited for everyone to rise and shine. 'Noah, go and knock on the bedroom doors and tell them all Father Christmas has been.'

AN HOUR LATER THE LIVING room looked like a bomb had gone off with wrapping paper strewn everywhere. The air was filled with the comforting savoury and slightly salty aroma of bacon sizzling as Mammy and Quinn whipped up a full Irish large enough to feed the Irish rugby team. Roisin was making a half-hearted attempt at picking the discarded paper up and putting it all in a rubbish sack. Noah was assembling a complicated new Lego Airport Control Tower, Cindy was perched on Pat's knee in pink pyjamas whispering in his ear, and Moira was engaged in a stand-off with Pooh. Aisling was setting the table, determined that they'd all squeeze around it somehow. She'd been delighted with Roisin's gift and even more so when she'd heard the story their American guest Gerry had told Roisin about his connection with Cliona Whelan.

'Oh, Rosi, do you think she'll meet him today?'

'I hope so, I really do.'

They would have to wait until later to find out.

Roisin put the rubbish bag down. She wondered how Shay's morning was unfolding in the cottage where his mammy had grown up. Then, with a sigh, she realised Noah should call his father before they sat down to breakfast and wish him a Merry Christmas. She'd telephone him now and get it out of the way. The phone rang long enough for her to wonder how she'd feel hearing his voice after her carry-on with Shay yesterday. Would she blush bright red hearing Colin's voice? Hearing him pick up and say, 'The Quealey residence,' however, she was surprised to find she didn't feel much of anything. It seemed she really had moved on. She exchanged pleasantries and tuned out as he blathered on about it being very quiet given it was just him and his mother. She would not feel sorry for him, not after enduring the pre-Christmas, Christmas dinner with them. When he mentioned it was looking like cheese on toast for their lunch, she interrupted and called Noah over, pleased when he snatched the phone from her, eager to fill his daddy in on all the things Santa had dropped down the chimney for him. He was also bursting to tell him about the copious amount of poo Mr Nibbles had done on his journey over.

WHEN THE CRY WENT UP as most of them were scraping their plates clean, Roisin was marvelling at Cindy's restraint in sniffing and only eating half the rashers on her plate. She'd never seen someone only eat the white of a fried egg before either. She was just thinking how well Patrick was doing out of it all, having seen him forking his girlfriend's discarded food onto his plate when the squeal made her drop her fork and spin around in her chair. The rest of the family followed suit.

Roisin registered two things; Noah was sitting on the floor next to Mr Nibbles cage, and the door of the cage was open.

'He's run away!' Noah wailed.

Now was not the time to ask him why the cage door was open, she decided, seeing his bottom lip was trembling and his eyes were beginning to fill up.

'Christ on a bike,' Moira said, the first to move. 'Come on, you lot, shift it.' There was a mass downing of cutlery as chairs were pushed back and the search began. Moira, who was surprisingly clear headed in emergency situations, took control ordering Cindy and Patrick to search their bedroom. 'Roisin you do yours and Noah's. Noah, see if he's hiding in the bathroom. Mammy, check ours. Quinn and Ash, you're on the living room and kitchen. And nobody is to leave the apartment. We've got a situation here that needs to be contained. Do you hear me?' Everyone nodded and nobody thought to ask Moira where she planned on searching, not when she was doing such a good job delegating. 'Right let's bring this gerbil home.' They duly head-ed off in the directions in which they'd been sent.

The sound of drawers slamming shut, wardrobe doors opening and closing, and audible groans as people stood back after being on their hands and knees searching under beds, em-anated throughout the apartment but there was no sign of the furry fellow. Roisin was feeling sick as she checked through their cases. She'd been so sure it was going to be a perfect family Christmas and now this had happened. He was so small, so vul-nerable, it didn't bear thinking about. She realised she'd gotten very fond of the little chap and would be as devastated as Noah were he to have met an unhappy end.

She appeared back in the living room in time to see Mam-my waving a piece of lettuce about making kissy-kiss noises as she called, 'Here, Mr Nibbles.' The only response was the thud of Pooh's stumpy tail on the carpet. Roisin looked at Pooh and was suddenly horror-struck. Surely not? He and Mr Nibbles were related. Well, in a pet uncle, nephew way at least. She wasn't sure she wanted to go closer for fear of him licking his chops and confirming her worst fears. She was going to have to though, they needed to know what had happened, to put to-gether the missing pieces of the puzzle.

She got down on all fours and crawled towards him. 'Have you something you want to tell me?' She didn't know what she expected the poodle to say. Should she suggest one woof for I did it, two for not guilty? As she drew nearer the tail thumping got more excited. He obviously thought she was playing some sort of game and he clambered off his bed eager to get things underway. Roisin gasped because there, curled up in the middle of the pillow, was a small brown and white furry ball. She carefully scooped up the bundle, hoping he hadn't suffocated under all that curly poodle hair but to her relief he was warm and on closer inspection she saw his eyes were closed. He was sound asleep she realised, rolling him back into his cage and closing it with a firm click before calling out that the search was over.

So it was, the O'Mara women and Cindy retreated down the stairs to the kitchen to begin their mammoth prepping session for the Christmas dinner with Mammy spouting off about Christmas miracles all the way. Aisling muttered a Christmas miracle would be if Patrick got off his arse and did the breakfast dishes while they were gone.

Chapter 28

Roisin untied the apron she'd donned and stood in the kitchen doorway, admiring last night's handiwork in the dining room. It was resplendent with glitzy tinsel and lots of it, along with screeds of paper chains. It looked very Christmassy, she decided, sniffing greedily at the aroma from the roasting turkey. The smell of it was like sliding under a comforting warm blanket on a cold winter's day, she thought. She'd never have believed she'd have room for Christmas dinner after the amount of food she'd tucked away at breakfast time but there was something about coming home to Dublin that always increased her appetite and the delicious whiffs from the kitchen were making her hungry once more.

Aisling had said the bird had another half an hour in the oven and then she'd get it out to rest. Mammy had crossed turkey off her list with flourish before leaning over Quinn's shoulder to enquire about the plum pud. 'Now be sure to add a decent splash of the cognac when you bring it through, Quinn,' she bossed. She'd been walking around, Santa hat slipping down over one eye, in her yoga pants as she clutched a clipboard singing along to Frosty the Snowman. A short, bossy elf as she kept an eye on the smooth running of the kitchen, eager to get everything on her list crossed off by the time Bronagh, Mrs Hanrahan, Nina and Tom arrived. She heard her call out, 'Moira, are your roast taties crisping?'

'Yes, and could we please listen to something other than your Foster and Allen Christmas collection? Oh, and, Mammy, don't forget to get changed before everyone arrives. The only person who should be in pants that tight is Tom.'

Actually, as Tom's rear flashed to mind, Roisin had to agree with her and she didn't fancy her chances of hearing the end of Foster and Allen. Her own jobs were finished, the smoked salmon starter having gotten the nod of approval from Mammy whose cheeks were looking flushed thanks to the mulled wine she'd insisted on sampling. 'You don't need a mugful, Mammy,' Roisin had protested to no avail.

'Look, Mummy,' Noah cried, spying her in the doorway. He held up a serviette folded into the shape of... a peacock? No, Roisin realised, the fanning tail was that of a turkey. The upset of the mystery of the missing gerbil was obviously long forgotten. Mr Nibbles and Pooh were both upstairs with various Christmas treats to hand so weren't missing out, but Pooh especially couldn't be trusted down here in the kitchen. Noah was sitting at the end of the table, one of six pushed together to make a long rectangular table in the middle of the room. Aisling had done a lovely job setting it. Cindy was sitting next to Noah and it was obviously under her tutelage he was learning how to make the turkey serviettes. 'It's a Thanksgiving tradition at home,' she drawled, blinding Roisin with her teeth.

'Well, you're doing a grand job the pair of you, they look fabulous. The perfect finishing touch to the table.'

She eyed Cindy who'd dressed with her usual leave-little-to-the-imagination flair, although she hadn't escaped being mammified. On top of her head she wore a Santa hat, as did they all. It was tradition, Mammy had declared. Looking at her brother's girlfriend she felt a cloud beginning to hover. It was threatening to blanket her good humour. She wondered if Patrick had been entirely honest with her as to his reasons for wanting to come home this Christmas. Because he certainly hadn't been honest with his sisters. She wished she hadn't overheard the conversation she'd heard earlier but she had and she couldn't unhear it now. It was down to the table's centrepiece that she had. The burlap arrangement of gingham ribbon and pine cones had been in the family for generations and Christmas wouldn't be Christmas if it wasn't on the table, Aisling had declared. 'It must be in the box we keep the Christmas decorations in upstairs. I think I put it back in the hallway cupboard, would you mind fetching it, Rosi?'

Roisin had duly trooped up the stairs of the ghostly guesthouse; silent as its guests had all ventured out for their Christmas dinners, and as she pushed open the door to the family's apartment, she heard Patrick's voice. She was about to call out when she realised he was talking to Mammy. She'd thought she was in the kitchen with Moira and hadn't noticed her leave. There was something in her brother's tone, a wheedling, smooth sort of tone that made her ears prick up. She wasn't the type to skulk about like Ita listening to other people's conversations and this one was clearly meant to be private but she was unable to move. 'Ten thousand will do it, Mammy. That will be enough to get the project off the ground and I'll get it back to you with interest before the year's out.'

Roisin shook her head. It seemed a leopard really didn't change his spots after all. She'd made a show of banging the door shut then and shouting out she was looking for the decorations box. Mammy had appeared in the hallway looking shifty although why she should be the one who looked like she had something to hide, Roisin didn't know. She wouldn't let on, she decided, as Mammy pointed her to the cupboard and said she should find it in there. She'd not breathe a word of Patrick pressing Mammy for money to her siblings, not today anyway.

Voices at the top of the stairs saw her push the cloud away and she moved to greet Bronagh and Mrs Hanrahan knowing the frail, elderly woman would need help getting down the stairs. She had indeed grown thinner but then it had been a long time since Roisin had last seen the sweet old woman. Her bones were like spindly twigs, she thought, being careful not to snap her as she hugged her hello. Her eyes held that same naughty twinkle ever present in her daughter's though. 'It's wonderful you could come and you both look gorgeous,' she announced. Mother and daughter preened.

'Ah, Patrick,' Bronagh said as he appeared behind them. 'You're just in time to help my mammy here down the stairs.'

'It's been a long while since I've been on the arm of a handsome young man. Hello, Patrick. The last time I saw you, you were still in short pants.' It was an exaggeration but they all laughed nevertheless and Patrick played the part of gallant escort to the hilt.

Tom was the next to arrive, a bottle of wine in each hand, which left him defenceless when Moira grabbed his backside by way of greeting. She said she was checking his pockets for her Christmas present but they all knew better. It earned her a telling off by Mammy but she wasn't deterred and homed in on him for a very merry Christmas kiss. Nina followed closely behind Tom. She'd brought a plate of sweets with her. 'They are called turrón,' she told them in her accented, precise English. 'It's a traditional Spanish nougat made with almonds we always have at Christmas.'

'It looks delicious, thank you.' Roisin said taking the plate from her and hoping by the end of the afternoon Nina would have lost the sad look that always lurked in her eyes. Bronagh exclaimed over the table and the decorations. Mammy fussed around seating Mrs Hanrahan and fetching her a cup of mulled wine.

It wasn't long before they sat down to a feast and Patrick kicked the festivities off by clinking his glass with his spoon and announcing he'd like to say a few words.

'Brown nosey fecker,' Aisling mouthed at Roisin, making her smirk. She wondered what he would have to say.

'Here's to O'Mara's, not just a family legacy but a family home. To O'Mara's.'

'To O'Mara's,' everybody chimed, and Roisin kept her whirling thoughts about her brother firmly under wraps. Nothing was going to spoil today, nothing.

THERE WERE CRIES OF that was delicious and oh, I'm so full as Roisin carried through the last of the dinner dishes to the kitchen and adding it to the mounting pile declared, 'I say the men do the washing up.'

'I agree,' Aisling said, soaking the oven dish, that had cooked the turkey to perfection.

'Here, here,' Moira piped up from where she was scraping leftovers into the bin.

'Ladies, away with you, I've a plum pudding to be sorting.'
Quinn herded them out and sitting back down at the table
Roisin looked down the length of it at the Christmas crackers
that had been pulled. The lame jokes had been read out to
groans and laughter and the Santa hats abandoned in favour of
paper crowns. The conversations bouncing up and down and
back and forth as they all awaited the arrival of pudding were
full of laughter and she could feel the love in the room. She
leaned back in her chair, tempted to clasp her hands over her
belly. She felt for the first time in a very long while, content.
This had been her year of second chances. She'd had a second
chance at life, love and now today this was her second Christmas. And it had been a very good Christmas indeed.

'CAREFUL YOU DON'T SET fire to the paperchain!' Maureen exclaimed. 'Where's the fire extinguisher?' The plum pudding was alight with blue flames and Quinn stood back triumphantly while everybody clapped.

'He knows what he's doing, Mammy,' Aisling said, offering
to help dish the dessert as the flames died and he began doling
the pudding into bowls along with a healthy dollop of cream.
He was quite sharp with her, Roisin thought frowning, as he
told her no, he could manage passing the first of the bowls
down the table.

Aisling looked a little put out too as she sat back down.
Quinn never took a tone with her.

'Is there money in this, Mummy?'

'I think there might be, Noah,' Roisin replied, tucking in.

'Mammy, watch your false teeth, we don't want any accidents,' Roisin heard Bronagh say as a jubilant shriek went up from Maureen who'd found five pence. Noah too was victorious but Aisling's reaction was a bit extreme, she thought, looking across the table at her sister who, annoyed at Quinn, had tucked in with gusto. Now her mouth was opening and shutting at a rate of knots as she said, 'Oh my God, I don't believe it. I just don't believe it.'

Was she crying? Roisin looked at her incredulously. Sure, it was only five pence!

'Oh, Quinn!'

This was getting ridiculous.

'Aisling, what's gotten into you?' Maureen demanded, pointing her spoon at her. 'If you've money worries you only have to say.'

Roisin didn't look at her brother.

'Yes! Yes! Yes!'

Was that a yes to the money worries? she wondered as everybody else stared at Aisling as though she'd grown a second head. What on earth was going on?

'Look! Look what was in my pudding!' Her cheeks flushed a pretty pink and her eyes flashed with excitement as Aisling held up a sparkling solitaire diamond ring for them all to see.

Roisin didn't know who screamed the loudest out of them all, Moira, Mammy, herself or Bronagh as the penny finally dropped. She pushed back her chair and raced around the table to hug her sister.

This really was a Christmas they'd never forget.

THE SOUND OF A BIN lid clattering to the ground startled Roisin from her sleep. It took her a moment to figure out what it was that had woken her up, but when her sleep fogged brain twigged she gently nudged Noah. He made a mumbling sort of a noise but she didn't give up, telling him to wake up because she knew he wouldn't want to miss out. 'We've got a visitor,' she whispered. 'Come on.' That stirred him and she pushed the duvet aside waiting for him to clamber out of bed first before getting up herself. They padded over to the window and Roisin pulled the curtains back, bracing herself for the polar blast as she opened the window just enough for them both to be able to peer down to the courtyard below. Just as she'd thought, illuminated by the sensor light and staring back at them was Mr Fox. The snow from Christmas Eve had melted now and the courtyard's paving stones glistened slickly.

'Mummy, should we go and get him some cheese?' Noah's whisper was loud on the silent night.

'No, no need, there's enough leftovers to feed a small army in that bin, so there is. Mr Fox is going to have himself a fine Christmas feast.' She hugged her boy close to her and they both watched as, having decided they weren't a threat, the little red fox nosedived into the bin. 'Do you think we should leave him to enjoy his dinner, Noah?'

Roisin shivered and Noah nodded, but before they closed the window he leaned out and called softly, 'Merry Christmas, Mr Fox,' before running back to their warm bed.

Epilogue

Clio strode into the foyer of the Merrion. She was still very much a trouser wearing woman and had chosen a simple lemon suit today that she knew suited her well. Oh, how times changed though, she thought, remembering how out of place she'd felt in the hotel the first time she'd come to meet Gerry here. Confidence was indeed a perk of age. She nodded a greeting to the concierge and only paused in her stride to sign her name with practised flourish, wishing the guest who'd run over book in hand— her book would you believe it—a Merry Christmas. She knew the way to the drawing rooms and it was as if time had stood still as she pushed opened the door. The chandelier still shone with rainbow light, the armchairs you could sink into and forget you ever had a care in the world still invited you in, and the fire crackled and spat to ensure you forgot all about the cold outside.

He was there, just as he'd promised he would be. He looked up as soon as the door opened, holding her in his clear and beautiful blue-eyed gaze. The smile, the dimples were the same, she saw, hanging back a moment, her heart threatening to jump from her chest. This was her chance to open herself up to the possibility of them rewriting their ending just as she had in her book. They could have their happy ever after because life was full of never-ending possibility and with that Clio stepped into the room, her face breaking into that goofy grin, the one she'd never been able to contain when she set eyes on Gerry.

The End

Read on to find out about the next book in the Guesthouse on the Green series...

Maureen O'Mara on behalf of herself and her late husband, Brian, requests the pleasure of your company at the marriage of her daughter,

Aisling Elizabeth O'Mara

To

Quinn Cillin Moran

A WEDDING AT O'MARA'S out Valentine's Day - 14 February 2020

If you'd like to be kept up to date with the wedding arrangements you can subscribe to Michelle's newsletter here via her website: www.michellevernalbooks.com[1]. To say thanks, you receive an exclusive O'Mara women character profile.

---

1.   http://www.michellevernalbooks.com